W9-ALN-155

Other Harper Junior Books by Barbara Robinson

The Best Christmas Pageant Ever
Temporary Times, Temporary Places

BARBARA ROBINSON

My Brother Louis Measures Worms

And Other Louis Stories

HARPER & ROW, PUBLISHERS
Cambridge, Philadelphia, San Francisco, St. Louis,
London, Singapore, Sydney
NEW YORK

My Brother Louis Measures Worms

Printed in the United States of America. For information address Harper & Row Junior Books, 10 East 53rd Street, New York, N.Y. 10022. Published simultaneously in Canada by Fitzhenry & Whiteside Limited, Toronto.
Typography by Joyce Hopkins
1 2 3 4 5 6 7 8 9 10
First Edition

Library of Congress Cataloging-in-Publication Data
Robinson, Barbara.
My brother Louis measures worms.

"A Charlotte Zolotow book."
Summary: Young Mary Elizabeth relates the humorous misadventures of her brother Louis and the other wacky members of her unpredictable, very odd family.
[1. Family life—Fiction] I. Title.
PZ7.R5628My 1988 [Fic] 87-45302
ISBN 0-06-025082-8
ISBN 0-06-025083-6 (lib. bdg.)

For my very special aunt, Jean Dodds

Contents

My Brother Louis Measures Worms

And Other Louis Stories

Louis at the Wheel

I was ten years old when my little brother Louis began driving my mother's car, and by the time I was eleven he had put over four hundred miles on it. He figured out that if he had done it all in one direction, he would have landed in Kansas City, although I'm not sure he allowed for rivers and mountains and other natural obstacles.

I also wasn't sure that my mother was really as astonished as she said she was when all this mileage came to light. And, in fact, she finally acknowledged that she probably knew what Louis was doing, but she just didn't believe it.

"It was like one of those dreams you have," she

told my father, "that seem so real when you wake up. Let's say you dream that the President of the United States shows up for dinner. And you say, 'Oh, I'm sorry. All we have tonight is meat loaf.' And he says, 'That's just fine, Mrs. Lawson. Meat loaf is my favorite. Do you cook it with bacon across the top?' "

She hurried right on before my father could comment on the story so far. "Now, when you wake up, you know it was a dream. You know perfectly well that the President of the United States didn't come to dinner, and isn't going to come to dinner. But if he *were* to come, you know, beyond a shadow of a doubt, that he would say, 'Meat loaf is my favorite. Do you cook it with bacon across the top?' . . .

"That's the way it was with Louis and the car—as if I dreamed that he was driving the car, woke up and knew absolutely that he wasn't . . . but if it turned out later that he *was*, I wouldn't be surprised."

My father said that was the wildest kind of reasoning he had ever heard in his life; that dreaming the President came to dinner had absolutely nothing to do with why Louis, at his age, was driving up and down the street and all over the place. He also said that anyone who dreamed about meat loaf probably needed to get up and take some Alka-Seltzer.

"Well . . . you don't like meat loaf," my mother said.

This was a good example of how her mind worked, and to say my father found the process mysterious is an understatement. He never understood her brand of logic, but at least it never surprised him.

Nor did it surprise him to learn, when the whole thing was sorted out, that it was Mother who first told Louis to drive the car—though of course she didn't say, "Louis, go on out and drive the car. Pull the seat up as far as it will go and sit on one or two telephone books."

Mother was not that casual about cars and people driving them, probably because she didn't learn to drive till she was almost thirty-five years old. As a consequence, she never enjoyed driving and would go out of her way to avoid it unless she absolutely had to go someplace and there was absolutely no other way to get there.

She was, therefore, dismayed when my father bought her a car for Christmas. It wiped out her number-one excuse.

"Now you won't have to depend on buses," he said, "or other people, or using my car. I hope you like the color. Do you like the color?"

Mother said she loved the color, that it matched the living room. This was very much on her mind because what she really wanted for Christmas was a new sofa, which would also match the living room.

My father led her in and out of the car, showing off its many features, while Mother oohed and ahhed, stuck her head in the trunk and under the hood and nodded knowingly at the mysterious innards coiled up there.

It was a difficult performance, since all she asked of a car was that it would start, keep going and stop when it was supposed to—and that she would not have to drive it very much.

But there was worse to come. Having provided Mother with the means of mobility, my father wanted to hear all about how she was enjoying it.

"Well, where did you go today?" he asked every evening, and he was always disappointed if she hadn't been off and running. So she had to lie, which she didn't do very well; or tell the truth, which was not what he wanted to hear; or hedge, by saying she was sick, or worn out or cleaning the oven.

In view of all this stress, it was probably not surprising that she should absentmindedly tell Louis to pick me up from my flute lesson on a day of complicated comings and goings. My father was out of town; Mother was leaving at noon with her friend Ada Snedaker to go to a flower show forty miles away; I had missed my regular flute lesson and, hence, my regular ride.

As we ate breakfast that morning Mother tried to work all this out: "If *I* drive to the flower show I could leave early and get you at your lesson—but I can't fit all the plants in my car. Your father won't be home till after nine o'clock. The *car* will be here but what good is that? I suppose Louis could pick you up, he gets home from school at three thirty. . . ."

"All right," Louis said, but nobody heard him—and of course my mother didn't really intend that Louis, not yet eight years old, should drive her car all the way across town and get me at my flute lesson. She was simply thinking out loud, dissecting a problem: people who must be picked up; plants which must be transported; cars in which to do all this; and people to operate those cars.

"Or you could take a bus," she suddenly said. "That's what to do. You get the bus outside Miss Cramer's house, and then transfer to the Mabert Hill line."

Satisfied with this arrangement, she put the whole thing out of her mind and went off to the flower show, or so I assumed. I was therefore surprised, while waiting for the bus, to see Mother's car coming down the street very slowly and, as far as I could tell, entirely on its own.

The car stopped about a foot away from me and a disembodied voice said, "Let me have your geography book."

It was Louis.

"What are you doing?" I said. "Are you crazy? You can't drive a car!"

"Yes, I can," he said. "It isn't easy, but I can do it—but I need your geography book to sit on so I can see."

I was too horrified to think straight. Never a rambunctious child, I was a born follower of orders and obeyer of the law, and here was my own brother running amok—or so it seemed to me.

The most puzzling thing was that Louis was not a rambunctious child either, and I couldn't imagine what had gotten into him.

"I just thought I should try it" was all he would say as we drove home . . . down back streets and alleys where no one could possibly see us. No one could possibly see Louis anyway, even sitting on my geography book. I wanted him to sit on my flute case too, but he wouldn't do it.

"Then I couldn't reach the pedals," he said, which was true.

Thus it began; for, since we were neither killed nor arrested in the course of this trip, it seemed to me, in retrospect, less harum-scarum than I first thought. And in no time at all, I accepted the fact of Louis at the wheel, as people *do* accept the most unlikely or bizarre circumstances if they happen often enough and nobody pays any attention to them.

It turned out to be a great convenience. If I didn't want to ride my bicycle to a friend's house, Louis would take me; if we ran out of peanut butter or notebook paper or Cheerios, Louis would go get some. On tiresome rainy afternoons we could go downtown, or to the library, or to the YMCA.

To be sure, we could never go very far or stay very long. There was always the remote chance that Mother would want to go somewhere in the car, or the equally remote chance that she would notice the car was gone and wonder why.

Of course, Mother's apathy about the car was our great ace in the hole. When absolutely necessary she would go do whatever errands had to be done; but at all other times the car simply didn't enter her thinking. For one thing, she was perfectly happy *not* to go anywhere, having dozens of puttery projects at her fingertips at any given moment. Then too, most of her friends were tremendous get-up-and-goers, car keys always at the ready, and they counted on Mother to go along—to lunch, to various sales, to flower shows and needlework exhibitions. So she was always busy, quite contented, and able to ignore the car for days on end . . . though she didn't want my father to know that.

Our other ace in the hole was Louis himself. He was probably the only eight-year-old boy alive who would drive all over town in his mother's car and never tell anyone about it, never see how fast he could go, never take a friend for a ride.

His attitude was never "Hey, look at me!"—so no one ever did. We might have been children and a car from outer space, touring the countryside unseen, which was a little spooky.

There were spooky aspects as well for my mother—unexplained peanut butter and Cheerios—but she tended to dismiss such minor mysteries on the grounds that she must have bought the thing, whatever it was. Being unwilling to run to the store for this or that, she shopped like a bear about to hibernate.

She could not, however, anticipate every whim.

"Do you know what I'd like?" my father said one evening. "I'd like some old-fashioned gingersnaps. They used to sell them in bulk, by the pound. They were hard—almost broke your teeth off."

Mother frowned. "I could try to make some, but I wouldn't make them hard, to break people's teeth off."

"Well, that's what they were," my father said. "Hard, like rocks."

The very next night, while rummaging around for something to nibble on, he found a big brown sack labeled *Old-Fashioned Gingersnaps*, which he brought into the living room for all of us to share.

"Well, where did you find those?" Mother said.

"I found them in the bread drawer."

"No, I mean where did you buy them?"

"I didn't buy them." He grinned at her. "Come on, Grace, I know you bought them, and I appreciate it. Here you go. . . ." He handed the sack to Louis and me.

"Don't break your teeth off," Mother said automatically, but her mind was clearly elsewhere, her eyes puzzled, as she tried to figure out how this sack of cookies got into her bread drawer all by itself.

"I bought them at that little store where they sell the airplane models," Louis told me later. "I used my airplane-model money."

"That was nice, Louis," I said.

"Well . . ." He shrugged. "I figure, I never buy any gas."

Of course, there was no way that we *could* drive up and buy gas; but we didn't have to, because Mother always bought gas whether she needed it or not. Since we knew this, and since we never went very far anyway, we didn't even think about gas. We also didn't think about other people using the car, since no one consulted us about such matters.

Consequently we didn't know that my father had used Mother's car on a Monday, when his was in the shop—and we didn't know that Mother's friend Helen Moulton borrowed the car two days later, when *hers* was in the shop.

So it was that on the following day, Louis, driving downtown, ran out of gas and, not knowing what else to do, simply left the car parked on Grandview Avenue. He carefully locked it up and walked home, a distance of some five miles.

Long before he arrived my father had come home, missed the car and, after a tangle of misunderstanding involving Mother, Mrs. Moulton's cleaning lady and Vinnie Tedesco at the service station (who seized the wrong horn of the dilemma and thought that *he* had mislaid *Mrs. Moulton's* car) called the police.

An officer came and took down all the information, much of it dealing with Mrs. Moulton, who was two hundred miles away in Cincinnati.

". . . and driving my car, probably," Mother said. "I *told* Helen to use the car. I didn't say when, or what for." Mother hadn't wanted to call the police at all, and was uncomfortable about the fuss being made.

"Well, Helen Moulton wouldn't drive your car to Cincinnati without telling you," my father said.

"When did *you* last drive the car?" the policeman asked.

Of course Mother didn't want to go into that

because she hadn't driven the car for two weeks, and she knew my father would be so exasperated with her, which he was.

They were both edgy and a little cross, but I was just scared to death because I couldn't imagine what had happened to Louis.

He arrived home eventually. After the police called to say they had found the car—undamaged, locked and out of gas. "Unusual for it to be locked," the officer said.

Louis, unaware of all this commotion, had automatically put the keys right back on the hook where they belonged and where they were discovered ten minutes later, to further complicate matters.

"How can the car be locked on Grandview Avenue, while the keys are here?" my father puzzled.

"Well—maybe Helen left them?" Mother suggested, but with little conviction.

"That would mean that Helen stole the car."

"Maybe you just didn't see them when you looked before?"

"That would mean that no one stole the car." He shook his head. "Well, I have to go get it before it rolls away all by itself. I wonder where on Grandview Avenue it is?"

"It's in front of the eye doctor's house," Louis said.

I had known, I think, that he was going to say this, or something equally damning. He was worn out from his long walk and only half awake and responding by instinct.

"Well, at least it's not the way downtown, but even so. . . ."My father stopped.

In the heavy silence that followed, Louis came to, realized what he had said and was, I suppose, too tired to wiggle his way out.

"I just ran out of gas," he said, which was true in every way.

We were grounded, of course, forever; and several other punishments were considered. But we were not easy children to punish, because of those very traits of character and temperament which had allowed us to drive around, unnoticed, for a year: our caution, our modest goals (in terms of destination), our quiet ways while motoring. Besides, my father seemed more inclined to blame himself, my mother and the public at large for failing ever to see what we were doing.

So, in the end, nothing much happened to us.

Mother, however, continued to fret. She seemed to think that Louis would now be driven to drive, as people are driven to drink, and saw the car as a dangerous temptation . . . or so she said.

I suppose my father saw no reason to maintain a car no one wanted to drive—except Louis, sitting on telephone books.

"Well, you'll be out one Christmas present," he told Mother. "So you have one coming. Make it a good one."

"Oh"—she eyed the sofa, which was old and rump-sprung and didn't match the living room—"I'll think of something."

The Mysterious Visit of Genevieve Fitch

Maxine Slocum lived two houses down from us, and when Maxine's cat got pregnant, Mrs. Slocum called up all the mothers in the neighborhood to say that all children would be welcome at the lying-in unless their mothers objected. It was the beginning of an enlightened era and no mother wanted to seem unenlightened, so everybody accepted Mrs. Slocum's invitation.

My father said it was the craziest idea he had ever heard in his life. "There must be thirty-five kids in this neighborhood," he said. "What are they going to do, put up bleachers?"

"They have that big basement," Mother said.

"Suppose the cat decides to have her kittens in the hall closet, or under the bed? Poor damn cat. . . ." He looked at me and my little brother, Louis. "Take my advice, don't go. Be kind to a cat. How would you like to have a baby in front of thirty-five people?"

"French queens used to have to," Louis said, "to prove the succession."

When Louis said things like that, people always raised their eyebrows and whispered to Mother that he must be a genius. He wasn't, though; he was just one of those people who remembered odd, unrelated facts. Ask him to tell you what "the succession" meant, and he would have been up a tree.

I was only worried that the cat would have her kittens in the middle of the night or something, but Maxine promised that if that happened she would run out in the street and ring her father's antique cowbell.

"Don't worry, Mary Elizabeth," she told me. "You'll hear that."

In the meantime, we all kept the cat, whose name was Juanita, under close surveillance and privately hoped to get a kitten out of the whole thing.

According to my father, that was really Mrs. Slocum's dark purpose. "It isn't that she wants to provide this rich educational experience for everybody under sixteen," he said. "She just wants to get rid of the kittens."

In any case, the approaching accouchement of the cat had us all in a state of fevered anticipation; and so when Genevieve Fitch took up her sudden and mysterious residence at our house, I was too preoccupied to wonder why.

This suited my Mother right down to the ground. The less said about Genevieve Fitch the better, in her opinion; but she had to make some kind of explanation because nobody else in the family was quite sure who Genevieve Fitch was.

Genevieve wasn't exactly a perfect stranger, but her relationship was so remote—third or fourth cousin, two or three times removed—that I had never before laid eyes on her, nor had Louis, nor had my father. But Mother was one of a large family with whom she tried to keep in some kind of touch, and my father didn't begin to know who all of them were. When strange relatives showed up from time to time he always made them welcome, but he didn't always remember, later on, just who they were.

Of course, when Genevieve showed up, he didn't know the nature of her predicament (or even that she was *in* a predicament), because Mother didn't tell him the whole story. She simply said that Genevieve would be staying with us for a few days while the inside of her house got painted.

Though this seemed odd—every three or four years the inside of our house got painted and nobody moved out—it was the kind of oddity that children can understand and accept. I had one particular dress that I would never wear on Wednesdays. Louis would eat no sandwich that was not cut on the diagonal. Genevieve Fitch would not stay in a house that was being painted. Who knew why?

After a day or two of Genevieve, my father decided that he would like to know why. Had she been a sprightlier person he might have been more willing to take Mother's vague explanation at face value . . . but Genevieve was a pale, somewhat doughy young woman with all the personality of wallpaper paste, and I suppose he was honestly bewildered that my mother, who had lots of snap and hustle, would be willing to put up with so flat a presence for so silly a reason.

"Does Genevieve always move out when her house is being painted?" he asked.

"I don't know," Mother said.

"Probably everything is being painted this time—walls, woodwork, ceiling—just one big mess all over the place. Easier to move out and let them get it done. Is that it?"

"Yes," Mother said, much relieved. "That's it."

But of course that wasn't it, and as new, puzzling scraps of information came to light, the plot thickened. We learned, for instance, that it wasn't Genevieve's house at all, but her mother's house; and that her mother, Ethel Fitch, was still in it despite the big mess all over the place.

We also learned that my mother and Genevieve had not seen each other for almost six years; and that, in fact, for the first few days of her visit, Genevieve had mistakenly believed herself to be visiting Cousin Olive Underwood and *her* family.

My father immediately saw the possibilities in this. "Well, it's all a big mistake," he said. "She isn't even supposed to be here. And this Olive Underwood cousin is watching and waiting for her . . . probably worried to death. We'd better get her packed up and take her there right away."

"No, no," Mother said. "Certainly not. Genevieve just got mixed-up. And you can't blame her. Look at you, you can't keep all my relatives straight either."

"Maybe not, but if I planned to move in with one of them, I would at least pick one I knew by sight."

Shortly thereafter he happened to run into one of the few he *did* know by sight, Mother's brother Frank, and Frank knew all about Genevieve.

"Good thing she could stay with you," Frank said. "Had to get the poor girl away from the smell of that paint, you know. Believe me, I gave her mother a piece of my mind. Not that it does much good. Ethel never did have any sense . . . crazy woman."

From this conversation my father deduced that Genevieve was seriously allergic to paint (the one interesting thing he had yet learned about her); and that her mother, Crazy Ethel, either didn't know or didn't care about her daughter's allergy. While he didn't like the sound of it, at least it was some kind of explanation.

In later years, when recalling the whole affair, Mother always insisted that she did not intend a deliberate deception; that she simply wished to spare my father the burden of Genevieve's problem. And she always pointed out that if he had ever asked her, flat out, "Is Genevieve pregnant?" she would have said, "Yes." But he never asked.

"Why in hell would I ask?" he always said. "Why would such an idea occur to me?"

Why, indeed? Genevieve, being shapeless and lumpy all over, didn't *look* pregnant, and nothing she ever said while living with us would lead to that conclusion. As for putting paint and pregnancy together, like two and two, my father would have come up with five every time, and when this danger was eventually explained to him—"The smell of paint can make a woman miscarry"—he said that sounded like something Louis would tell us without knowing what he was talking about.

Nevertheless, Genevieve was pregnant, and respectably so, though temporarily abandoned by her husband, one Leroy Fraley. This was Mother's initial understanding of the situation and though, like my father, she didn't like the sound of it, she did feel sorry for Genevieve. She felt the press of family obligation, however far removed, and she agreed with Frank that Ethel Fitch didn't have good sense. (In fact, this was a substantial understatement. Ethel was definitely closet kin: not quite loony enough to be committed, not quite sane enough to run loose.) Most of all, Mother believed that Genevieve's stay would be brief, her departure orderly, and that, in the meantime, efforts would be made to locate the footloose Leroy Fraley.

All of this added up to "Genevieve's problem," from the burden of which my father was to be spared, much as he was spared all sorts of minor domestic dilemmas. Mother never called on him to manage things that she could manage herself or to sort out awkward situations that, left alone, would sort themselves out. Besides, she knew that he would find the tangle of Genevieve's affairs preposterous, and she was afraid that he would object to having the whole thing dropped in his lap . . . or, to be precise, in his spare bedroom. He recognized that there were unfortunate people all over the place who couldn't seem to regulate their lives, but he didn't expect to find any such people under his own roof.

Of course, he didn't count sickness as mismanagement. It wasn't Genevieve's fault she was allergic to paint, he felt, and in the absence of anything else to talk to Genevieve about, he talked to her about her "condition."

"I know you get a very serious reaction to this," he said, "but just how does it affect you? Do you break out in a rash? There's a young woman in my office who has your same trouble, and her face swells up. She can't see, can hardly eat. . . . It's a terrible thing. Has that ever happened to you?"

"No . . ." Genevieve said, looking pretty worried. "But my feet swell up if I'm not careful."

My father said that was most unusual, he had never heard of that. "I understand the worst of all is the respiratory effect. These people who suddenly can't breathe . . . their throats just close up—" and then, as Genevieve looked *really* worried, he went on, "I'll tell you what you ought to do—you ought to get a shot. You know, they have shots now for people like you. But you don't want to wait till you're in trouble. You want to get the shot well ahead of time. Then, too," he added, "they can make tests and find out just what causes this condition."

"Oh, I know what causes it," Genevieve said.

"Not necessarily. It could be any number of things. It could even be something you eat."

From this, and similar cockeyed conversations,

Genevieve apparently concluded that my father was just as crazy as her mother, so it's no wonder that she grew restive for Leroy Fraley to come and take her away.

She mentioned this once or twice to Mother—"I surely do hope that Leroy can come pretty soon"—but Mother never knew what to say in reply, it seemed like such a pitiable state of affairs. It never occurred to her that Genevieve might know where Leroy Fraley was, until, in desperation, Genevieve decided to join him.

She had overheard the tail end of a conversation between Louis and my father, in which Louis asked how many kittens Juanita the cat might have. My father said that under the circumstances—the great publicity, the Slocums' damp basement and a cast of thousands—it would be a miracle if she had even one, and a greater miracle if that one didn't have to be taken away from its mother and drowned.

"Why would it be drowned?" Louis said.

"Well, maybe not drowned, but put out of its misery. Sometimes it's kinder. If it isn't healthy and vigorous, it won't survive anyway, and it's just better to do away with it."

It was this last speech that Genevieve overheard, and so harsh a view, coupled with my father's seeming belief that pregnancy was caused by any number of things, including diet, and that it could be prevented by inoculation, apparently convinced her that she had gone from a frying pan into a fire and had better get away while she could.

"But, Genevieve, where will you go?" Mother said.

"I'm going to Leroy. He can't come here, so I'll go to him."

"What do you mean, he can't come here?" Mother wanted to know. "And how can you go to him, if you don't know where he is?"

"I know where he is," Genevieve said. "He's in Latticeburg, Kentucky. He's in jail."

Mother certainly hadn't counted on this, but it did fit in with her notion of a man who would desert his pregnant wife. She called Frank with the news, and Frank said he would find out about it right away. He also said that Genevieve must stay right where she was; the smell of paint in Ethel Fitch's house was still too strong for safety.

This was very discouraging information for my mother, who by this time felt herself hopelessly caught in an intrigue for which she had no taste in the first place, and little aptitude. But there wasn't anything she could do about it except wait—for the paint to settle or for Leroy Fraley to be sprung, whichever came first.

The next day Frank called, sputtering over the telephone, to say that he had found Leroy and that Leroy was in jail for stealing a car—specifically, the car of Ethel Fitch.

"He says he borrowed it," Frank said. "She says he stole it. I believe him, because he doesn't sound smart enough to steal a car, and we all know Ethel's crazy. Either she lent it to him and forgot she did, or she lent it to him and had him arrested anyway. I don't know why she would do that, and I don't much care. I'm going to get him out of jail if I can and get him back here. He *wants* to come back. He loves Genevieve."

Mother, reeling from this series of fresh alarms, seized on the one bright spot. "It's wonderful that he feels that way," she said. "I'm sure everything will work out, and he can be with Genevieve when the baby comes."

In view of the imperfect communication on all sides, it's not surprising that nobody knew exactly *when* the baby was supposed to come. My mother assumed that it was due in four or five months because that was what Frank assumed—on the testimony of Ethel Fitch, who had told him something about Genevieve being "all set by the middle of September." Genevieve must have known when the baby was due; but since she had never even mentioned a baby to Mother, Mother assumed that she was unhappy about it or ashamed about it, and she didn't want to hound Genevieve with painful questions.

Consequently, when Genevieve went into labor, nobody knew what was going on, including Genevieve, who was expecting a monumental stomach-ache and did not associate low back pain with the onset of birth. She suffered in silence all day, and by the time she finally decided that this must be something more than muscle strain, things were very far along.

My mother hardly knew what to think. She had heard of miscalculation, but never of miscalculation by five months.

"But Genevieve," she said, "isn't this baby coming much too soon?"

"Not for me," Genevieve said.

Then there was the problem of my father. Having hoped to keep him in the dark about the whole thing or, at the very least, to surprise him with the news sometime next year ("You remember Genevieve Fitch? Well, Genevieve has a lovely baby!") Mother now had to bring him up to date in a hurry.

"Will you bring the car around front while I call Dr. Hildebrand?" she called downstairs. "We're going to have to take Genevieve to the hospital."

"What for?" he shouted up. "What's the matter?" And then, still believing Genevieve to be the victim of allergy: "I'll bet it was those oysters we had for supper, wasn't it?"

"You don't understand," Mother said. "Genevieve isn't sick. She's having a baby . . . this very minute."

My father, however shaken and mystified by this announcement, apparently recognized the urgency of the situation. For one thing, he could hear Genevieve moaning from upstairs that she dare not try to move. "Never mind the car," he said to my mother. "I'll call an ambulance. You see what you can do for her. I'd better call Hildebrand too." A few minutes later he rushed up the stairs. "Is there anyone else I should call?" he asked.

"You might call Frank."

"I was hoping there would be a husband I could notify."

"He's in jail," Mother said. "I couldn't tell you. You would have had a fit. You know you would. Did you reach Dr. Hildebrand?"

"He's on his way. Also the ambulance. Didn't you think I would catch on when this particular moment arrived?"

"Yes," Mother said, "but this baby is five months early." She did not add that this was Frank's estimate.

It was hours before the whole thing got straightened out, and in the meantime Juanita the cat escaped from the Slocums' basement and disappeared, and all the neighborhood children (summoned by Maxine ringing the cowbell) ran up and down the street and in and out of everybody's yards looking for her.

Amid all the clamor Genevieve had an eight-and-a-half-pound boy upstairs in the bedroom. She did it all by herself because the ambulance arrived too late and Dr. Hildebrand was busy trying to improvise some kind of incubator for what he believed to be a dangerously premature birth for a seriously allergic mother. But then he got most of his information from my father, who was, in this case, the worse possible source.

Eventually all the loose ends got tied up. Leroy Amos Fraley, Jr., being of great size and marked vigor, was obviously not even five minutes early, and Genevieve's allergy was only a figment of my father's misinformation.

Ethel Fitch, on hearing the good news over the phone, said it was the end of all her hopes and dreams for Genevieve, which had involved a three-month course in beauty culture, to run from mid-June to mid-September (which took care of another loose end) and a subsequent career of styling hair in the front room of the Fitch house. Why else, Ethel wanted to know, did Mother think she had embarked on this painting-and-decorating project? She had done it, she said, all for Genevieve, who had repaid her by taking up with a convict.

My father, trying hard to catch up, said that, crazy or not, Ethel had a point. "After all, " he said, "this Leroy *is* in jail, isn't he?"

"Yes," Mother said, "but only because Ethel lent him her car and then said he stole it."

At this point the ambulance, having shut its door and gone away, returned . . . with Juanita and four kittens.

"Didn't like to put 'em out in the street," the driver said, "and we figured they must have come from somewhere around here."

"Bring them right in," my father said. "We seem to be in the business."

Juanita the cat hung around our house for two or three weeks, much to Maxine Slocum's disgust; Louis and I got to keep one kitten, which we named Leroy in honor of the day's events; and Genevieve and the baby stayed with us for four days until Leroy, who had been released from jail, arrived to take them away.

We all stood around on the front porch watching them go, and my father said now that it was all over he felt like a man who had wandered into someone else's home movie and then wandered out again without ever knowing what it was all about. Louis and I felt much the same way. While watching and waiting for Juanita to have kittens, we had missed the main event; had overlooked the forest for the trees, so to speak, and then missed the trees too.

But, happily for us, there remained one final confusion.

"What do you mean, Leroy is going to have kittens?" my father said the next spring. "How can a male cat have kittens?"

"Well, we were wrong about that," Mother told him. "And since all the children were so disappointed last year when Juanita ran away, I thought I might call just a very few mothers and see whether their children would like to come—"

"No," my father said. "No . . . no . . . no."

Louisa May and the Facts of Life

Mrs. Slocum's plan to expose us all to the facts of life came a little too late. Everybody in our neighborhood had already been exposed to them, although we didn't know it at the time, and didn't understand that sex had reared its ugly head right across the street in the unlikely person of Louisa May Fuller.

Louisa May and her sister Alma lived on the corner in a little gray cottage, and were described by my cousins from Elyria as "crazy old maids." But Louis and I had known the Fuller girls all our lives, and didn't think they were very strange.

"Not strange at all," my father often said, "compared to some of your mother's family."

Alma was the older of the two, and therefore the head of the family, so she made all the big decisions, like how to get ready for Judgment Day. Louisa May decided what to have for dinner and when to paint the house. Louisa May did the washing and the cooking; Alma did the needlepoint and cross-stitched pretty thoughts on all the dish towels. Louisa May scrubbed the kitchen floor and waxed the furniture; Alma picked up the living room and straightened the doilies.

They both were officers of the Women's Missionary Society—Louisa May rolled bandages, made layettes for African babies, collected and mended everybody's used clothing for the mission boxes and kept careful track of the organization's funds; Alma was in charge of devotions every other month, which accounted for most of the pretty thoughts on the dish towels. However, despite this lopsided division of labor (or maybe because of it), they got along very well, agreeing on almost everything except Alma's special concern: a great passion for searching out and recording the genealogy of the Fuller family, which was a matter of very little interest to everyone else, including Louisa May.

After much correspondence, Alma would establish a family tie with somebody in Ponca City,

Oklahoma, or East Orange, New Jersey; and she would throw up the window and sing out the news to Louisa May in the garden. "Mr. Fuller, in East Orange, is a third cousin twice removed!" she would call, hoping vainly for some enthusiastic response. But Louisa May just didn't care about all these far-flung connections and considered Alma's fascination with the subject a terrible waste of time, and a little silly into the bargain.

"It's not as if we came from anything grand," she used to tell my mother, "and even if we did, what would be the good of knowing it?"

Louisa May's hobby was babies. She adored babies. To be sure, noboby in the neighborhood was known to harbor an active dislike of babies, but Louisa May went to the opposite extreme, and seemed to view each individual baby as the beginning and end of all human wonder. Wherever a new baby appeared, there too was Louisa May, hard on the heels of the doctor.

My mother was fond of her, and she worried about her. "Louisa May," she would say, "you ought to get married. It's just a shame, the way you love babies, that you don't have a family. And you don't want to wait forever. You're thirty-eight years old and it's time you had your own babies. Now, you just find some nice man and marry him."

"Oh, Mrs. Lawson," Louisa May said, "I don't

want to get married and have to fool with some old man around the house."

"But he wouldn't be old!" Mother insisted. "You want a respectable young man who's a good provider."

"Well, I don't want any young man either," Louisa May always said. "I don't know. . . . Sometimes I ask myself, Would it be worth it to put up with a husband so I could have a baby? But I just can't seem to decide it would. Alma and I have our own ways of doing and things go along pretty smooth, and I wouldn't want to bring a stranger into the house."

Louisa May's predicament was not openly discussed at home because my mother was particular about discussions of babies and how to get them. But my father was equally particular about having all of us under his nose at the supper table, and at least two or three times a week he missed my little brother Louis.

"I suppose Louisa May Fuller has got him again," he would grumble. "Why in hell doesn't Louisa May get married and have her own children and quit borrowing Louis?"

Of course this was partly Louis's fault—he loved to have Louisa May borrow him because she let him eat raw cookie dough and ride around on her vacuum cleaner.

"Louisa May doesn't want to get married," Mother said. "She doesn't want to fool with a man around the house."

"Well, she could fool with one long enough to get some babies, and leave mine alone."

I didn't see my mother kick him under the table, but I saw him wince, and the subject was changed to some less interesting topic of the day—less interesting to me, at any rate. Louis wouldn't have cared, because he was only five years old, but I was almost eight and just barely smart enough to know that there were mysteries beyond my ken, and that one such mystery had to do with babies.

I concluded that there must be mysteries beyond my father's ken, too, in view of his remark; for if I didn't know anything else about the subject, I did know that the only way in the world to get a baby was to get married. All the available evidence supported that conclusion. In the first place, that was what I had been told; and in the second place, no unmarried ladies of my acquaintance had babies. Like most little girls, I shared Louisa May's enthusiasm and took it for granted that if there were some other way to get babies, everybody would have a few—my schoolteacher, Miss Lincoln; my Aunt Blanche; Miss Styles, who worked at the grocery store; Louisa May, of course . . . maybe even Alma.

I was therefore both amazed and delighted to

discover that I was wrong when Louisa May—though still unmarried—got a baby.

Not all at once—she took the usual length of time. But since Louisa May was so large and so comfortably padded, it was five months before her condition began to arouse speculation . . . and another month before Alma noticed anything amiss.

Then Alma brought my mother half of a coconut layer cake. "Too bad to have it go stale," she said, "and Louisa May and I can't eat it all up—or shouldn't, anyway. I've noticed of late that Louisa May is putting on weight, and I try to help her curb her appetite."

Louis and I loved the cake and ate most of it feeling sorry for Louisa May who apparently *couldn't* eat it.

"Just because she's fat?" Louis shook his head.

Naturally there was gossip, but it was sketchy and disorganized. There was nothing anyone could put a finger on, so to speak, until one day when Mother quite innocently called across the street, "How are you, Louisa May?"

Louisa May came right over, beaming. "Oh, Mrs. Lawson, I feel wonderful, and I'm just going to tell you why because I know you'll be happy for me. I thought a lot about what you said—about getting married and all, and especially about being thirty-eight and not waiting too long; and, Mrs. Lawson, I just got afraid to wait anymore."

"Oh, I'm so glad," Mother said, puzzled but relieved.

"I knew you would be. I don't know what Alma will say. She's not as crazy over babies as I am, and I just know she'll think I should have got married anyway, but"—and Louisa May shrugged—"this opportunity came along and I just thought, Well, why not?"

My mother was speechless. In her moral firmament there existed good women and bad women, and though she had never personally known any bad women, she had a clear image of how they looked and behaved. They would be gaudy, she felt, and rough and coarse, with brassy hair and low-cut dresses. Louisa May, on the other hand, was as plain, and as good, as homemade bread.

Furthermore, Mother had a vague, uneasy notion that she herself had somehow aided and abetted this state of affairs.

Alma turned out to have the same notion. At some point she took a good look at Louisa May and realized that her weight problem was neither permanent nor proper, and she came charging across the street to accuse Mother of encouraging immoral behavior.

"I didn't encourage her," Mother said. "I never said it was all right. I just wanted her to get married."

"Oh, how lovely that would be!" said Alma

hysterically. "But she didn't, and just see the fix she's in, and she's not even ashamed a little bit. I don't know what in the world to do!"

Mother felt sorry for Alma. "Maybe she could go away somewhere. . . ."

"She won't. She says they might take the baby away from her but that old Dr. Barney will let her keep it, and he will, he will! You know how soft he is, and what will I do?"

This didn't make much sense to Louis and me but we were glad Louisa May didn't have to go anywhere she didn't want to go.

"She won't say who the father is," Alma went on. "She says it's none of my business. She says—" Here Alma choked. "She says he was a nice man and for me not to worry about it."

Mother was so flabbergasted by the whole affair that she had no shock left to spare for this, nor even much curiosity, and my father seemed torn between outright astonishment and a kind of grudging approval on the grounds that he would no longer have to hunt around for Louis.

Louisa May did in fact fail to exhibit the least shred of shame or regret and she did not go away somewhere, but she did oblige the neighborhood by staying within doors as much as possible until her baby was born. It was a boy, which was what Louis had said it would be, but he did not claim any special credit for this.

Louisa May bought a very expensive imported perambulator, and what little time she was not feeding the baby, bathing him or rocking him, she wheeled him up and down the street with a rose stuck through the roof of the carriage, humming little tunes and literally commanding people to see how beautiful he was. She called him "darling" and invited other people to call him that too until she hit upon exactly the right name for him.

Nobody needed a second invitation to view the baby, so great was the curiosity as to his parentage. No baby was ever scrutinized more carefully for identifying features, nor with so little satisfaction—for when he got to look like anybody at all, it turned out to be Louisa May: a distinct disappointment to all.

That was later, though. For the time being he looked pretty much like most babies: plump, bald, rosy. He was an unusually happy baby, which prompted someone in the neighborhood to remark, "Love babies always are"—although on the face of it, Louisa May's baby hardly fell into that category. He was so happy, I suppose, because Louisa May didn't allow anything to make him unhappy, and his healthy good humor was almost an affront to decent, respectable women whose babies were fussy or fretful or colicky or pale or cross-eyed.

Won over by the baby and influenced by Louisa

May's own attitude (she simply ignored the whole question of the baby's beginnings, as if he had just appeared one day out of thin air), most people quit trying to sort out the moral issues of the case. Reverend Seagraves was asked by one or two of his flock to please call upon Louisa May, and did so, but with no clear purpose in mind and no visible result. Had Louisa May sought counsel, he would have counseled her; had she sought comfort, he would have comforted her; but as it was, all he could do was hold the baby while Louisa May cut him a quarter of a Gravenstein apple pie and read him recent correspondence from the missionary in Bechuanaland.

He ended up by offering to baptize the baby on the first Sunday of the month, although, as he said, he wasn't sure how the congregation would feel.

He need not have worried. Nobody expected or wanted the baby to suffer, and even the most puritanical of the parishioners seemed to take the view that here was a baby who *needed* to be baptized. For most people, though, there was a less lofty consideration. Since the baby didn't *look* like anybody, they pinned their hopes on having him *named* for somebody, and there was every indication that church attendance on that Sunday would set new, towering records.

My mother was shocked by this. "There are

people planning to go to church this Sunday," she said indignantly, "who haven't been inside the church since *they* were baptized!" At first she said she wouldn't go, and then she said my father wouldn't go, and then Louisa May asked both of them to stand up with her and be the baby's godparents, which delighted Louis and me.

My father said at least that way they would be sure of getting a seat, which made Mother so mad that she didn't speak to him for over an hour. It was no joking matter, she said.

It was not, to her. My mother's moral code was simple, uncompromising and, up to now, uncluttered by doubt. She believed that virtue is its own reward and that the evildoer will reap the whirlwind, but Louisa May had scrambled these precepts. Besides, Mother loved Louisa May and didn't want her to reap any whirlwind. Neither, though, could she ignore what was a clear and definite lapse of virtue.

She agreed to be the baby's godmother because she knew Louisa May wouldn't ask anyone else, and she felt it would be compounded cruelty to deny the baby honorary parents when he didn't even have a full complement of real ones.

I was thrilled about the whole thing because I thought it would give me an in with the baby, and he was so generally admired that his good favor amounted to a juvenile status symbol. Neither I nor any of my friends understood exactly how Louisa May came to have him, and though we wondered about it, we didn't wonder nearly as much as our parents thought we did. We just assumed, variously, that he had been brought by a stork, found under a pumpkin or left on Louisa May's doorstep by a band of gypsies, and we really didn't much care.

On the morning of the baptism we were about fifteen minutes ahead of time, but already the church was filling with people. "The baby has a lot of friends," I whispered to Louisa May, and she smiled.

Father, Louisa May with the baby on her lap, Alma and I all sat together in one pew, saving a place for my mother. She and Louis were coming with our neighbors the Pendletons because there wasn't room in our car, and as the organist started the opening hymn my father began to look around and mutter, "Wonder what's become of her?" I tried to see too, but there were too many people. It was my feeling that Mother was probably stuck back at the door, unable to push her way through, but then I saw Mrs. Pendleton, with her hat on crooked, steaming down the aisle.

She leaned across me and said, "Louis stuck a bean up his nose and we had to take him to a doctor. They're still there. You'll just have to go ahead without her." She started away and then turned back. "Louis is all *right*, you understand. It's just that—"

"He stuck a bean up his nose," my father said. "I see. Thank you."

The hymn over, Reverend Seagraves came down out of the pulpit to the baptismal font.

"Never stuck a bean up his nose before," I heard my father mutter as he stepped out of the pew and started to follow Louisa May up the aisle. I was sorry for Mother, who was going to miss what I considered her big moment, but very proud of my father, who was going to stand beside Louisa May and assume responsibility for her baby before God and man and our entire congregation and a considerable number of total strangers.

I guess the same thought occurred to him, because he stopped three rows up, and then, after a moment's pause, came back and got me. "You come too, Mary Elizabeth," he said "You can take your mother's place."

Poor baby, to be represented by such a group. Only Louisa May seemed to be in full possession of herself. Reverend Seagraves was trying to sustain the shock of the unexpected size of his congregation, and to overlook the appearance of a distinctly minor child as a baptismal sponsor. I assumed that Louisa May would hand me the baby, according to the usual procedure, but instead she handed him to my father, who looked very much surprised and immediately handed him to Reverend Seagraves, who also looked surprised, because he already had his hands full. But I suppose he didn't like to hand him on to anyone else—especially not back to my father, who had almost dropped him the first time around.

Louisa May, however, remained perfectly serene, and at the appropriate moment pronounced the baby's name as if it were as common, say, as Charlie.

It was not, and all those who had hoped for revelation in the naming of this baby had their hopes dashed. Louisa May named her baby Hannibal—a name never connected with anybody or anything in our community. It was her one indirect concession to public opinion, for surely, all things being equal, she would have preferred a name more natural to the ear. But she offered neither explanation nor justification for the name, except to say that Alma thought there might once have been another Hannibal Fuller way back in the genealogy. Alma hadn't thought any such thing, but she liked the idea of it so much that she came to believe it was true, and from then on spent most of her time trying to track him down.

My father hurried us away right after church, and Louisa May let me hold Hannibal on the way home. He was soft and warm and sleepy and probably quite uncomfortable, smashed against my bony chest.

"Will you tell him someday that I'm his godmother?" I asked.

"Well, more like godsister, maybe," Louisa May said. "Oh, yes, I'll surely tell him."

"I'll take him to school when he's old enough," I said, "and Sunday school. I'll watch out for him."

"I count on you," she said.

The excitement of the day, the weight of Hannibal upon me, the warmth of the sun through the window of the car, all made me as drowsy as the baby.

"Where did you get him from?" I asked.

Alma gasped. "Why, we went out one morning to fetch the milk . . ." she began.

"Not quite," Louisa May said, and then to me, "The where and the how is a mystery. As for the why, just say I wanted him a whole lot, and was old enough to take good care of him."

My mother was home from the doctor and waiting for us. "I took a taxicab," she said. "There was no use going to the church so late. How did it go?"

"Well . . ." Father sat down heavily on the living-room sofa. "You can just about imagine . . . everybody and his uncle there in the church. I walked right past the Ferguson brothers. Saw Amos Ball a couple of pews over. Ed Wiggins . . ."

"Oh, well," my mother said.

"Oh, well? Comes the big moment and who walks up the aisle with Louisa May and her baby? Me! By myself."

"Well, people must have known . . ."

"What? That Louis stuck a bean up his nose? I doubt it. Besides, there were people there who don't know me from Adam's off ox—perfect strangers." He took out his big white handkerchief and mopped his forehead. "Worst spot I ever was in. Then Louisa May gave me the baby and I didn't know what to do with him."

"Why didn't you give him to me?" I asked, and Mother stared at me.

"Where were you?" she asked.

"I was there too. I went up with Daddy. I'm Hannibal's godsister."

"Hannibal?"

"Hannibal," my father repeated, and shrugged. "Well, she couldn't very well name him Frank, or George, or Bill."

"She could have named him Fred," I said, "for you."

He mopped his head again. "I thought of that.

Oh, yes, that occurred to me while we were standing up there."

I was sent upstairs to change my Sunday dress and heard only a snatch of their conversation: ". . . have to tell her *something*, I think. Louisa May told her it was all a mystery . . ." When I returned my father had gone out to look at the garden and Mother was sitting by the window, reading a church bulletin. She was holding it upside down.

"Come and sit down," she said. "Your father told me you asked Louisa May where she got her baby . . ." Poor Mother, she made hard work of the facts of life. By and large her remarks only served to confirm what Louisa May had said—it all sounded most mysterious, but more practical than finding babies under pumpkins, which had always seemed careless to me.

"Then Louisa May is bad?" I said when she was finished.

"Well, more misguided. Louisa May will have a hard time bringing up her little boy with no husband to help." I could see the sense of that. Certainly, I thought, I would want a husband to do all the things my father did around the house, but I didn't think Louisa May felt that way about it.

"Louisa May never wanted to put up with a

husband around the house," I reminded my mother.

"Well," she said, after thinking for a moment, "that comes of not knowing. Marriage isn't just a matter of putting up with a husband around the house. It's a kind of sharing of everything . . . good and bad, hard and easy. It's having someone who cares, to care about. It's ever so many things, and when Louisa May says she doesn't want to be married I expect she means it. But it's like saying you don't want any candy when you've never had any."

Later that day Mother and I made a freezerful of peach ice cream and took it across the street, and we all took turns giving Hannibal his first taste of summer in a spoon. I watched Louisa May cuddle the baby, putting her cheek against the downy softness of his head, and I still thought it strange that my mother should feel sorry for Louisa May when Louisa May so plainly didn't feel the least bit sorry for herself. But if, as Mother had said, her contentment came of not knowing, I was glad she didn't know.

We started back across the street when it was beginning to get dark, and my father came to meet us. "I told you to call over," he said. "That freezer's too heavy for you."

"Oh, it's almost empty now," Mother said.

"Still too heavy." He took the freezer from her,

pretending to stagger under its weight until Mother slapped him lightly on the arm. "Now you stop that," she said, laughing. "Why, people will think you're drunk. Now, stop. I mean it. . . . Oh, you!"

I lagged behind to catch lightning bugs for Louis, but I could hear them laughing all the way into our house, and even after I had gone to bed.

Big Doings on the Fourth of July

My mother—though a person of quiet ways and simple tastes, primarily interested in meat loaf recipes and January white sales—was prone to accidents of fate which landed her, time and again, in unusual, vaguely dangerous, or downright loony circumstances.

She was usually able to get herself out of whatever tangle she was in, but every now and then she had to call on my father, who said the same thing every time—"I'll bet this was your sister Mildred's idea"—which, very often, it was.

They were an odd pair, I always thought, to be associated at all, let alone as sisters, for they were as different as ducks and owls. They didn't even look alike—Mother was small and fair and conservative in matters of dress and makeup, while Aunt Mildred was a very tall and solid woman with dark hair and eyes—impossible to overlook, since her taste in clothes ran to gypsy colors and extravagant use of fringe and beads and trailing scarves.

Even Louis, who was only nine, thought that one or the other must have been adopted.

"Which one, Louis?" I asked him, but he said he didn't want to know because he liked them both.

"Now what does that mean?" my father said. "Does he think that in such a case you could only keep one—like puppies?" He shook his head. "Well, certainly Louis isn't adopted. He sounds just like your mother explaining why she went downtown on a bus to buy new curtains and came home in a taxicab with a vacuum cleaner."

"I couldn't very well haul that big awkward thing home on the bus," she had told him, as if that answered everything, which of course it didn't.

Pressed for further details, Mother said that she had, in fact, bought curtains at one store; subsequently found different, prettier, cheaper curtains at another store; returned the first curtains and bought a bedspread to match the second curtains. She then ran into Aunt Mildred ("Aha!" said my father) who was in hot pursuit of eiderdown pillows advertised on sale somewhere, though she couldn't remember where.

They joined forces, tried on some hats, stopped for lunch and then proceeded down Main Street, in and out of stores, looking for Aunt Mildred's sale pillows, which they never found.

Along the way, however, they were reminded of other homey needs and picked up what Mother called "a few things." The vacuum cleaner came from the Baptist Church thrift shop, where Aunt Mildred made a purchase similar in terms of unwieldiness: a concrete birdbath for her Oriental garden, which was, strictly speaking, neither Oriental nor a garden, but a collection of ugly outdoor statuary and a stunted crab apple tree.

They then called not one, but two taxicabs, so Aunt Mildred could use one of them to take old Mrs. Tipton home from the thrift shop and see her safely in her house. Aunt Mildred also took all the soft goods they had accumulated—curtains, bedspread, assorted dish towels and cotton underwear and needlepoint yarn—while Mother conveyed the birdbath and the vacuum cleaner, stopping on the way home to leave the birdbath in Aunt Mildred's garden.

"There, now," she said, at the end of this lengthy account. "Is that so terrible?"

"No," my father said, "but it's silly—you and Mildred running all over town in buses and taxicabs, loaded down with packages. Why didn't you take my car?"

"I don't like to drive," Mother said. "You know that."

"Why didn't Mildred drive?"

"Why, I don't know. It isn't as if we *planned* to go shopping. We just happened to meet."

Actually, Mother *did* know, but didn't like to say, that Aunt Mildred's car was in the repair shop again.

In matters of transportation, as in all other ways, they were exactly opposite. Mother hated driving cars, but when called upon to do so, she performed with caution and common sense. Aunt Mildred, on the other hand, loved to drive anywhere, anytime, with such zest and zip and freewheeling independence that she could be said to be unsafe at any speed.

It was for this reason (and others) that my father took a dim view of Aunt Mildred's plan to dress herself and Mother up in old-fashioned costumes and ride a tandem bicycle in the Fourth of July parade, for which, as chairman of the town committee, he was responsible.

Aunt Mildred said that Louis and I could dress up too, and ride our own bicycles beside or behind them, and we would all be a charming addition to the parade.

"I can't ride a bicycle," Louis said. This was unusual in a small town where everybody rode bicycles—but then, Louis was unusual. My mother once said that she believed Louis was born forty years old, and he did indeed have an air of solemn deliberation better suited to an adult. This kept him out of a lot of trouble—by the time he'd considered all the pros and cons of sneaking into some movie we weren't allowed to see, the movie was half over—but it also cramped his style, I thought, in matters of simple enjoyment, like riding a bicycle.

He'd considered the pros and cons of this, tried it in a dogged, down-to-business way, fallen off harder and quicker and more often than seemed reasonable to him, reconsidered and said he'd rather walk.

"Can't ride a bicycle!" Aunt Mildred said. "Why, it's the easiest thing in the world. . . . You know how a newborn baby will swim if you throw it into the water? Well, it's the very same thing—it's instinct."

I didn't think it was the same thing at all and neither did Louis, and my father said it would be a cold day in August before he threw any newborn baby into the water, just on Mildred's say-so.

He also continued to grumble about the proposed bicycle act—probably because he saw too much similarity between Aunt Mildred on a tandem bicycle and Aunt Mildred in a car, both being vehicles and subject to collision—but there wasn't much he could do about it, because there were signs all over town urging people to *Join the Celebration! Sign up for the Big Parade!*—and they were *his* signs.

"Mildred's just trying to help," Mother said. "Isn't that what you said you wanted—more people in the parade?"

"Yes, but not Mildred! I want Charlie Baker at the bank, and Floyd Gemperline at the Select Dairy—*business* people, to show some spirit and spend some money and enter some floats, so we'll have something to judge besides the V.F.W. and the Ladies' Hospital Auxiliary."

"Then you should have said so," Mother told him.

"I doubt that Mildred even has a tandem bicycle—and what makes you think she knows how to ride one?"

"Oh, of course she does; she was a very athletic girl," Mother said; but in fact she wasn't at all sure of this, and was somewhat lukewarm about her own role in the whole thing. Unlike Aunt Mildred, Mother was uncomfortable about any kind of public display—choosing always to dish up the dessert rather than introduce the speaker—and didn't really want to put on a lot of old petticoats and a floppy hat and ride down Main Street in a parade.

Furthermore, she had, at different times and in an offhand way, invited various relatives to a picnic supper on the evening of the Fourth; and since Mother was one of a large family this had gotten out of hand. She had mentioned some of the arrangements to my father—"Carl and Ava are coming over after the parade"; "I told Linnea and Walt to stop by for some fried chicken"—but she had not spelled out for him the exact dimensions of the guest list, which, when she added it all up, came to forty-seven people.

She had even invited my father's only sister, Della, to come from Zanesville, a hundred and fifty miles away—but she didn't tell him that, either; because Della, though always invited to festive occasions, never came—too far to go, she always said, and too hard to get there.

My father both understood and approved of this attitude. He was fond of Della, he said, and she was fond of him; but their family affection didn't require them to see each other every fifteen minutes, like most of Mother's relatives.

All in all, the Fourth of July looked like a complicated day, and Mother wasn't sure she wanted to begin it on a bicycle.

Louis, however, had no doubts at all. At my

urging, he made one last determined effort to ride my bicycle the length of the driveway, landed five times in the forsythia bush and said, once again, that he would rather walk.

My father, pleased by the response to his signs—nine floats, two high school bands, a drum and bugle corps, and a team of horses from the local Grange Association—was too involved with the logistics of the parade to notice that Louis was a little black and blue, or that Mother was frying chicken and peeling potatos from morning till night. But he did notice when she showed up at the dinner table wearing a pair of voluminous ladies' bloomers.

"Mildred got them somewhere," Mother said, "and I just feel so foolish that I thought I'd wear them around and try to get used to them. She said they'd be more practical than long skirts."

My father was so surprised and impressed by this display of good sense in Aunt Mildred that he changed his tune, and said the the bicycle would probably be a nice touch.

"I'll put you in right behind the drum and bugle corps," he said, "so no one will miss you."

The tandem bicycle which Aunt Mildred produced on the morning of the Fourth did not in fact belong to her, just as my father had predicted. It belonged to old Mrs. Tipton, who had put it out in the trash and was dismayed to find it still there on the day Aunt Mildred took her home from the thrift shop.

"Oh, they didn't take it!" she had said. "Now what will I do with the old thing?"—and of course Aunt Mildred had known just what to do with it.

"I had it tuned up," she told us, "at the repair shop where I always take my car."

"But that's an auto body shop," Mother said, eyeing the bicycle with justifiable suspicion.

"That's what they said," Aunt Mildred agreed, "and they didn't really want to do it; but with all the business I give them they couldn't very well say no."

She was dressed, as were we all, in a motley assortment of attic discards: petticoats, automobile dusters, ladies' shirtwaists of a bygone day . . . and hats as big around as turkey platters, but nowhere near as solid. Mother's hat was especially limp, falling down around her ears and almost to her chin, while Aunt Mildred's hat looked like a wedding cake; roses and feather birds and yards of trailing tulle.

Louis had suffered himself to be decked out like Buster Brown, in knickers and a straw boater, just as if everything was going according to plan. He reasoned that there would be no time, at the last minute, for Aunt Mildred to commandeer a bicycle, put him on it and throw him into the water, and he was right.

"You ride right in close behind us, Mary Elizabeth," Aunt Mildred told me. "We don't want to be strung out all along the street if we can help it. It's just a shame about you, Louis. You wouldn't want to climb up here with your mother and me?"

Louis said no, but if we didn't go too fast he would try to keep up with us on foot.

"Oh, we won't go fast," Aunt Mildred said. "You don't go fast in a parade. Grace, are you going to get on?"

"Where?" Mother said, holding up the front of her hat and hitching at her bloomers.

"Doesn't matter—front or back."

"Whoever's in front has to steer," I said.

"Well, you'd better do that, Mildred." Mother straddled the bicycle. "I'll pedal."

"You both have to pedal," I said. Louis and I looked at each other, aware now of what we should probably have known all along—that neither one of them knew how to ride the thing, and, even more surprising, neither one of them seemed concerned about it.

When asked about this later, Mother said she based her confidence on pictures she had seen of people riding such a bicycle—smiling, unruffled, hardly exerting themselves at all—and she concluded that two people on a bicycle produced great stability, no matter who the two people were. Of course, she realized almost at once that she was wrong about this.

Parade or no parade, Mother and Aunt Mildred had to go fast because that was the only way they could stay upright . . . and I had to go fast to keep up with them, as they swooped back and forth across Main Street, narrowly avoiding things and people, pedaling furiously or not at all, and never in unison.

Aunt Mildred seemed to be steering, after a fashion, with all her customary abandon; and Mother—resigned, as she later said, to six months in a body cast—was simply hanging on for dear life, unable to see much because of her hat.

Of course the rear rank of the drum and bugle corps was aware of all this, and though they continued to bugle and drum, they also tried to step up the pace of the march—torn, I suppose, between a desire to maintain order and a desire to stay clear of this runaway bicycle and its hapless operators.

In the meantime, my father, assured that all the floats and bands and marching units had started on time and in position, had gone on to the reviewing stand, where he had been much complimented on the organization and variety of the parade so far.

"Just fine, Fred," the mayor had told him. "Any surprises coming up?"

At that moment the police chief stood up and pointed down the street. "Something going on down there," he said. "That band's all over the place."

"That band"—the drum and bugle corps—was indeed all over the place, and for good reason. Aunt Mildred, increasingly hampered by the collapse of her hat—roses and birds were dangling from all sides of it, and she was nearly strangled by loose tulle—had suddenly yelled, "Look out . . . we're coming through!"

As the musicians scattered, my mother saw ahead the team of horses from the Grange Association. It was almost the only thing she had seen so far, and it was certainly the most hopeful, for the horses were hauling a low flatbed trailer carpeted with hay, in which sat three or four teenagers.

"Mildred!" Mother yelled. "Now listen to me! . . . We're going to jump. Come on, those kids will catch us."

Many of the onlookers seemed to think that this was a legitimate comedy act and applauded, but my father stood frozen to the spot, for what he saw was Mother and Aunt Mildred—"No mistaking *them*," he later said—jumping from their bicycle onto a hay wagon, while the bicycle itself crashed into the reviewing stand and died there, like a worn-out horse.

I did not see their landing, only their leap, and I dropped my bicycle and ran ahead . . . while Louis, puffing and panting, out of breath and wobbly-legged, rose to the occasion as people often do in moments of crisis. He got on my bicycle and rode to the hay wagon, thus accomplishing out of fear what he couldn't accomplish any other way.

Nor were we the only astonished and terrified family members: We passed a woman being helped to a seat on the grass, while people assured her, "I'm sure they're all right. I'm sure they aren't hurt." This woman looked pale and shaken . . . and vaguely familiar.

It turned out to be Aunt Della, who had arrived, unbeknownst to anyone, just in time to watch the parade. She had spotted Mother—not very hard, in view of the circumstances—had seen her take off in what looked like a suicidal leap through space, and immediately concluded that, through a cruel twist of fate, her first visit would turn out to be funereal.

That was also my thought, and I was relieved to find both Mother and Aunt Mildred safe and sound, though choking and sneezing from clouds of hay dust.

Since the whole thing took place directly in front of the reviewing stand, there was some talk of giving first prize to this combination float and acrobatic stunt, but my father refused to make any such award, on the grounds that it would encourage the prize winners to further lunacy.

He was so torn between relief and exasperation that he had very little emotion to spare when he arrived home to find the house, the yard, the front porch and the back porch full of Mother's relatives eating fried chicken and potato salad, except to say that it looked like a convention. He did, however, take Mother aside to tell her that if he heard Aunt Mildred say one more time, "All's well that ends well," he would not be responsible for his actions.

"You could have been killed," he told her. "You know that, don't you?"

"But we weren't," Mother said. She wanted him to look on the bright side: the great success of his parade; Louis, now riding my bicycle up and down the driveway with all the confidence of one who has slain his personal Minotaur; Aunt Della, at last present and part of a family reunion ". . . and having a wonderful time, too," Mother added.

"Should have come long ago," Aunt Della said. "Just got set in my ways, that's all. Don't you get set in your ways, Fred. Have a little fun, have a little excitement."

"It's not always the same thing," he said; and then, "Why didn't you say you were coming? I'd have met you at the bus station."

"Didn't come on the bus," Aunt Della said. "I came in a taxicab."

"From Zanesville?" My father stared at her.

"Well, I didn't start out to come *here* in a taxicab. I started out, you see, to go spend the day with my friend Audrey Wilson. Normally I wouldn't go *there* in a taxicab either, but I was taking along three dining room chairs for Audrey's nephew to repair, and then there was the quilt we're making for the church bazaar . . ."

Even to Louis and me, this was beginning to sound like bedspreads, curtains and vacuum cleaners all over again, and I could see from my father's face that he thought so too.

". . . said I was his last fare, that he was going to Piketon to spend the day with his brother, and I said *I* had a brother living not twenty miles from Piketon . . ."

Aunt Mildred had drifted over by this time and was listening with interest.

". . . just thought, oh, why not? It's the Fourth of July, after all. But don't worry, Fred, I don't expect to drive down here in a taxicab very often."

"Surely not," Aunt Mildred chimed in. "Della, I just love to drive, and Grace and I . . ." She put her arm through Aunt Della's and led her over to where Mother was dishing up potato salad, and they all fell into animated conversation, of which we heard only one snatch: "We'll just drive along, and see what we can find to do. . . ."

Louis wondered what happened to the dining room chairs and the quilt, and I wondered whether Audrey Wilson was still waiting for Aunt Della to show up at her door, but my father didn't ask about those details.

He just stood there, shaking his head and muttering to himself. "Three of them," I heard him say. "From now on, there'll be three of them."

The Wedding of Willard and What's-her-name

Of Mother's great swarm of relatives, my father had no special favorite and no special bête noire because, he said, they were all alike—and all perilously close to crazy.

They really weren't, of course, day in, day out. But he seldom saw any of them day in, day out, pursuing their ordinary rounds of activity. He saw them, instead, in great numbers, on holidays or on occasions of family celebration, all talking at once and recalling past events: "Remember when Louella blew up the beer?" ". . . when Ralph left the baby on the bus?" ". . . when Blanche brought the convict home for supper?" Details were never spelled out, and though my mother sometimes tried to fill them in for him, she usually made the whole thing sound even worse.

"Well, Ralph got off the bus in Chillicothe to go to the bathroom," she would explain, "and the bus went on without him."

"Went on to where?"

"To Columbus. He was going to Columbus."

"Ralph was going to Columbus?"

"Yes, but he got off in Chillicothe to go to . . ."

"Yes, I understand that. What about the baby?"

"The baby went on to Columbus on the bus."

"But didn't Ralph tell someone? Get them to stop the bus?"

"Why, he didn't know what to do, poor little thing. He was only—oh, I don't know—eight or nine years old."

"Eight or nine years old! What was he doing on a bus with a baby?"

At this point in the story—in any story—Mother's recollection would fizzle out. "I just don't remember," she would always say, "but there must have been a good reason for it."

It was a miracle, my father often said, that so many of them had lived to tell these tales; and he only hoped that my little brother Louis and I would learn something from all the mistakes in judgment.

We did, of course, learn some things—not to hobnob with convicts, not to leave babies on buses—but, despite my father's hopes, we continued to stumble into exactly the same kinds of dilemmas and to solve them, or not solve them, in exactly the same ways.

When Louis won the magazine contest, it didn't look at first like a dilemma at all, but like a great triumph. Louis entered magazine contests all the time and had never won anything, so I was very excited. Louis, mysteriously, was less so.

"It's just the second prize," he said.

"But, Louis, second prize is always something good! It's honorable mention that gets the soap and the dog food. What did you win?"

"I won a wedding." He read from the letter: " '. . . flowers, reception, bridal wardrobe, limousine . . .' and some other things. Three thousand dollars worth of things. *First* prize was a honeymoon in Paris, France."

I couldn't believe that when Louis finally won a prize it would be a wedding. "Why did you enter this contest, anyway?"

"I didn't know what it was. I found the entry blank on a table at the dentist. The top was torn off, so I just filled it out and sent it in." He looked at the letter again. "The magazine's called *Bridal Daze*."

"Daze is right," I said. "You'll have to write and tell them you're nine years old, so you can't use the prize—unless they'll keep it till you're old enough to get married, but I don't think they'll do that."

"I can't write to them," he said. "There's a place on all the entry blanks where it says 'I certify that I am twenty-one years old.' They'll arrest me."

"I don't think so," I said.

"They'll yell at me. Besides . . ." he looked stubborn. "I won the prize. I ought to get something."

"Louis, face it. This prize is for someone who wants to get married. Maybe you can trade it to someone who wants to get married."

Louis stared at me for a minute and then he nodded. "You're right," he said. "I'll give it to Willard."

That sounded perfect to me. Willard Armstrong was my mother's cousin, and our favorite relative. He gave us rides in his truck and took us to the movies, and he always sent us birthday cards signed *Very truly yours, Willard Armstrong.* Besides, he was grown up, he had a job and a girlfriend and—most of all—he wanted to get married.

Even my father liked Willard, though with reservations. He thought Willard lacked gumption and let people walk all over him. Mother said he didn't mean "people"—he meant Willard's girlfriend, Janine, who was also called Althea and sometimes Ginger, depending on what she said to call her.

"I like to try out all different names," she told

us once. "You can change your name, you know, if you don't like it."

"Don't you like your name?" Louis asked her.

"I like it better than I used to, but I'm not crazy about it." Janine whipped out a compact, rearranged one or two curls, and studied her face carefully. She did this a lot—hoping, we assumed, to suddenly hit upon exactly the right name to go with what she saw in the mirror. "I don't want to make a mistake though. I was all set to change it to Rosalie but I'm glad I didn't, because now I hate the name Rosalie. I may change it, or I may not, but I want to be sure."

When my father heard about this he said it was clear to him that Janine, or whatever her name was, must be a member of Mother's family, so it was no wonder that she kept turning down Willard's marriage proposals. "Doesn't want to marry her own third cousin," he said.

"That's the only thing," I told Louis. "Willard wants to get married, but Janine doesn't."

"Why not?" he said.

"I don't know why not."

"Maybe she doesn't want to get married till she knows for sure what her name is going to be—because, once Willard says 'I, Willard, take you, Janine . . .' that would be it, wouldn't it?"

My mother said no. "You marry a person," she said. "You don't marry a name. No, your father's right—Willard is too easygoing. Janine always has some silly reason why they shouldn't get married, and Willard just won't put his foot down. I don't know what will finally persuade her.'"

Louis and I thought we knew: three thousand dollars worth of flowers and food and limousines and bridal wardrobe, especially the bridal wardrobe.

Besides trying on all different names, Janine liked to try on all different clothes, and we never saw her in the same outfit twice. She said she had to look her best at all times because of her job at Kobacker's, where she sold ladies' dresses. "Besides," she said, "I get a discount, and it would be wasteful for me not to use it."

"I don't think they sell wedding dresses at Kobacker's," I told Louis, "and she probably doesn't have enough money to buy one somewhere else, because of using her discount. That may be one of the reasons she won't marry Willard."

Willard said he didn't think that was it. "I surely *hope* that's not it. No—Janine is just a very cautious person. Look how she is about her name. She's been trying out names ever since I've known her, which is six years. She doesn't want to make a big mistake—and I admire that." He sighed. "Of course, six years is a long time."

"I still think you ought to tell her about the

prize wedding," I said. "She might not want to waste it. You know how she is about her discount."

"Well . . ." Willard nodded. "There's that, all right."

Two days later Janine had set the wedding date, reserved a country club, located an eight-piece orchestra and gone off to Cincinnati to get fitted for a wedding dress.

We learned about all this from my mother, who was pleased for Willard but mystified by the arrangements. "I don't know what's the matter with her," she said. "Why, that country club's thirty miles away! What's wrong with the V.F.W. hall? And when your Aunt Rhoda called to say she'd make the wedding cake, the way she always does, Janine said she would take care of that because she wants a cake with a waterfall and continuous music. Rhoda said, 'Good luck.' I think she's crazy."

"Of course she's crazy," my father said. "Here's a grown woman who hasn't figured out what her name ought to be. Willard better think twice."

"Willard's had six years to think twice," Mother told him, "and all he can think is Janine."

It all seemed very romantic to me. "Just think, Louis," I said, "if you hadn't won your prize and given it to Willard, he'd still be waiting and thinking."

As it turned out, that had occurred to Willard

too, and it bothered him enough to discuss it with my mother.

"Of course, I know a nice wedding is important to a girl," he said, "especially a girl like Janine, who has to think about her appearance and all . . . and I don't really believe it was just the wedding that brought her around to say yes. You know, Janine doesn't make up her mind in a hurry."

"No," Mother said.

"I believe, though, that she'd about *decided* to make up her mind—and then, here came this wedding. And, naturally, she didn't want to see it go to waste. That's what she said. She said, 'Willard, we can't let this go to waste.' "

At this point, Mother realized that she must have missed something somewhere in the conversation, and that, in fact, it was not even the conversation she originally assumed it to be—a discussion about expenses, and the relative importance of certain details, such as musical wedding cakes—and wet ones, at that. She had planned to suggest that Willard put down, if not his foot, at least a toe or two, and rein Janine in a little bit. Now he seemed to be saying that Janine was doing the whole thing out of frugality.

". . . should think she'd be running out of ways to spend three thousand dollars . . ."

Mother didn't miss that. "Three thousand dollars! Willard, surely Janine doesn't have three thousand dollars—*you* don't have three thousand dollars, do you?"

"I guess not!" Willard said. "Nowhere close."

"Then where's it coming from?"

"Why—from Louis," Willard said.

It had not occured to him that Louis's prize was a secret, nor had it occurred to Louis and me that it *should* be a secret.

Louis said that if anyone had asked, "Did you win a magazine contest?" he would have said yes; and if they had asked, "What did you win?" he would have said, A wedding . . . and if they had then asked, "What are you going to do with a wedding?" he would have said, Give it to Willard.

"But nobody ever asked," he told my father.

"But, Louis, why in God's name would we ask—out of the blue—if you'd won a magazine contest?" Once again, my father said, we were up the river without a canoe; and, as usual, the details were buried in fog. He turned on Willard. "Why didn't you say something about this?"

"I did," Willard said. "When Aunt Grace asked where the money was coming from, I said, 'From Louis.' "

"But Louis doesn't have three thousand dollars!"

"I know that!" It was interesting to hear Willard raise his voice, even a little bit, because he never had before. "It isn't Louis's money, it's Louis's prize."

"It is not Louis's prize! Louis is nine years old. This magazine isn't going to give Louis the prize, so he can't give it to you!"

Willard thought about that for a minute. "I believe you're right," he said.

"In the meantime," my father went on, "Janine has been out ordering dresses and flowers and cakes, to the tune of three thousand dollars. So she's either going to have to come up with the money or call off the dresses and the flowers and the cakes."

Willard shook his head. "Janine's not going to want to do that. Why, she doesn't even like it when people return things at the store because they've changed their minds. You know, Janine's slow to make up her mind, but when she does . . ."

"Now, Willard," Mother said. "Listen to me, because I'm all out of patience with Janine's cautious ways. You just tell her that she doesn't need to drag us all thirty miles to a country club to hear eight perfect strangers play fiddles . . . and she doesn't need to drape the church from stem to stern with orchids, which Mr. Herms the florist doesn't know where he's going to get them all, anyway. She doesn't need any limousine to ride two and a half blocks, either. She doesn't need any of those things . . . now, you just tell her so."

To everyone's surprise (including his own, I guess) that was just what Willard did.

He told Janine to cancel the reception and the orchestra and the orchids and the cake, and to find some dress closer to home.

He never did tell her what happened to Louis's prize.

"Don't know why I didn't," he told my mother. "That would have been the place to start. But it seemed like when I left here I was mostly worried, and by the time I got to Janine's I was mostly mad. And then, right off the bat, she told me we had to have a lot of white doves to fly around outside the church. *Had* to have them, she said. So I knew right then that this whole circus was a big mistake, and I just told her we weren't going to have any part of it."

He did give in about one thing, though. He told Janine that she could go ahead and get her wedding dress if she would give up forever all thoughts of changing her name, because he didn't want that hanging over him for the rest of his life—and Janine, astonished, perhaps, by the demonstration of strength and purpose, agreed to everything.

It all turned out so well that my father had a hard time getting Louis to see the error of his ways, and Mother was no help.

"If Louis hadn't won the wedding," she said, "they probably wouldn't be getting married."

"Exactly," my father said. "Is that a reason to get married?"

"No. That's why it's such a good thing that Louis didn't *really* win the wedding. Willard would always wonder if that was why Janine married him, and now he knows it isn't."

My father sighed. "Now, this is typical," he said. "Louis has done a foolish thing and caused everyone a lot of trouble, and you seem to be saying that we should congratulate him. But just because this turns out all right doesn't mean that he can go on doing foolish things. When Ralph left that baby on the bus, it turned out all right, but . . ."

"Well, it did and it didn't," Mother said. "We got him back, of course—but I don't know how much babies remember. Maybe somehow he always remembered that he got left on a bus and taken to Columbus, and it affected his personality. Maybe he's never had much get-up-and-go because that scared it out of him."

"Who?" my father said. "What are you talking about?"

"Why . . . Willard."

"Willard! Willard was the baby Ralph left on the bus?"

Of course this was big news to Louis and me, and we could hardly wait to go find out whether Willard did, in fact, remember the experience, because Louis always claimed *he* could remember being a baby and could remember that he didn't much like it.

My father was amazed. He made Mother tell him the whole story again, and when she was finished he said it seemed even worse now that he knew who the baby was.

He also said there was probably no way to keep Louis's wedding out of the family history—"Remember when Louis was nine years old and won the wedding?"—but he did hope there would be someone on hand to fill in the details.

Trn Rt at Chkn Frm

Until Mother's mysterious malaise, my father had always believed her to be somewhat disorganized in her thinking but perfectly sound of mind—and when, for a brief time, he had reason to doubt this, it affected his own common sense.

"I was too worried to think straight," he said—and in the absence of *his* common sense and straight thinking there was no one in charge of the store, so to speak, and misunderstandings multiplied.

At first Louis and I didn't even know Mother was supposed to be sick—but, of course, Mother didn't know it either.

"I just wish I had known," she said later. "I

would have gone to bed with a lot of magazines and all the Perry Mason mysteries and had some pleasure out of it."

My father said she didn't deserve to have any pleasure out of it, that she had put him through a terrible time of strain and worry.

"I didn't put you through anything," Mother said. "You put yourself through it, being so secretive. If you thought I'd gone crazy, why didn't you say so?"

That was, indeed, exactly what he thought; but it was not what he told Louis and me, out of respect for our tender years. He simply said that Mother wasn't feeling well: that she might seem nervous and edgy, and we should try hard not to upset her.

We knew what that meant, or thought we did, and immediately began to wonder whether the baby would be a boy or a girl, and—since we were always bone honest with each other—whether we would like it, whatever it was.

We thought it odd that no one gave us the straight dope on the matter, babies being commonplace around the neighborhood and their origins no longer any special mystery. But we didn't think it was any big secret . . . and so, unwittingly, we complicated the whole misunderstanding.

I said something about our new baby to Mother's sister Rhoda, who, having just been told that Mother was in a precarious mental state, immediately put two and two together and got six.

She decided that Mother, then thirty-nine years old, either was pregnant and didn't want to be, or wanted to be pregnant and wasn't—and, in whichever case, had retreated from reality.

Aunt Rhoda also thought it odd that my father had not given *her* all the facts, but put it down to a sense of delicacy, this being so personal a matter. She also decided that if my father, a wholly practical and forthright man, couldn't even bring himself to suggest the details of the situation, she shouldn't say anything to him about it and must simply bide her time, be available and await developments.

Mother, unaware of all this, thought it odd that Rhoda should suddenly start dropping in every other day for no good reason, but finally concluded that she was just lonely or bored or maybe feeling old before her time. So, while Aunt Rhoda was watching Mother for signs of pregnancy and/or mental collapse, Mother was watching Aunt Rhoda for signs of despondency about her fading youth.

"Come with me to Circleville to judge a flower show," Mother would say, thinking that was just what Rhoda needed.

"Isn't that a long way to go? I don't think all this travel is good for you; you look tired to me. Why not stay home and rest?" Aunt Rhoda would say, thinking that was just what Mother needed.

As a matter of fact, Mother thought it was a long way to go, too. She loved the flower shows and the sociability and the tea and cookies, but she didn't love getting there.

My father had again provided her with a car—for his own peace of mind, he said, lest in some emergency she find herself crashing through traffic with Aunt Mildred—but Mother still had little confidence in her driving skills, and no sense of direction at all, and continued to avoid any expedition which required her to drive very far or to figure out where she was going.

Still, when elected a judge by her garden club, Mother must have decided that the pleasure involved outweighed the perils. Once or twice a week, at the height of the flower show season, she would set out, clutching maps and instructions on how to get to the appointed place in Circleville or Athens or Wilmington, but even so, she was either lost or late most of the time until she stumbled on a way out of this continual dilemma.

While she was traveling down the highway one morning on her way to a distant flower show, a sudden gust of wind blew her vital information out the window, leaving her stranded; because, as she said, "If I get lost with a map in my hand, I would certainly get lost without one."

At that moment she noticed a station wagon

ahead of her on the road—loaded with green growing plants, driven by a lady in what looked like a pretty hat; and, having nothing to lose, she simply followed this car on the reasonable assumption that it was going to a flower show.

"And not only was it going to the show," she added triumphantly, "but that lady won first prize for her tuberous begonia. It wasn't a hat after all, it was a tuberous begonia."

Thereafter Mother spent less time studying her maps (which didn't seem to help much anyway) and more time studying the traffic around her, with surprising success. Time after time she was able to locate, identify and pursue some member of the local flower show crowd . . . and thus arrive at the right place, on time and unruffled. Sometimes the clues were obvious: many plants, ladies holding dried arrangements; sometimes more subtle: a horticultural society emblem in the window, a bumper sticker reading *I Grow Gladiolas.*

Of course, my father had no idea that this was going on. He knew that Mother liked flowers and was a judge of them, but he had no interest in such activities. If she enjoyed doing it, whatever it was, he was happy for her, and that was that . . . and Mother, knowing this, chose not to bore him with details.

He was very much surprised, therefore, while having lunch with a customer in a town some forty miles from home, to look up and see Mother in conversation with the cashier of the restaurant—getting change for a dollar, as it happened, so she could use the phone in what was an emergency situation.

She had followed a car absolutely loaded with flowers and greenery all the way to its destination, which turned out to be a funeral home. She was not only distressed but somewhat indignant, because the driver of the car, a florist, had not used his delivery truck, in which case she would not have followed him in the first place.

My father excused himself to his customer and went to see what this was all about. Had anyone asked him that day about Mother's whereabouts he would probably have said, "Oh, Grace is at home—not much of a gadabout, you know," for so he believed.

"Well, this is a surprise," he said, and kissed her. "What are you doing in Fredonia?"

In Mother's reply lay the crux of the whole ensuing tangle . . . for what was she to say? That she had, by mistake, followed a car full of plants to a funeral home? That she was really supposed to be in Semperville, ten miles away? Most of all, that this was not a unique experience?

Various harmless fictions crossed her mind—she had come to visit a friend, to get the dining room chairs reglued, to buy something big and important on sale that very day in Fredonia—but Mother was no good at fictions, harmless or otherwise. An uneasy liar, she always fell apart two sentences into the lie.

However, it seemed to her that any answer involving the truth of this situation would surely lead to lengthy explanations, and might well produce some kind of public scene.

Hoping to avoid all this, she simply said, "I don't know," and immediately hurried back to greet the customer, to make polite small talk and to leave before my father could pin her down.

He said later that she seemed distracted, not herself, her eyes vague and troubled (all perfectly true, since she was then half an hour late for the flower show and had no idea how to get there). He was puzzled by her answer, but not alarmed . . . until the same thing happened several days later.

Mother had pursued what looked like a sure thing: an elderly Packard, gleaming clean and bearing three ladies in hats. They led her to a high school auditorium—a common flower show arena—and took from the back of their car three different flower arrangements, all of which turned out to be table decorations for a luncheon-lecture on Yugoslavian folk art.

Mother didn't know that, though; it looked to her like a flower show, and a very fancy and elegant one, which pleased her. She sat down at a table to make preliminary notes: *Good use of daisies in Number 7. Awkward larkspur in Number 10.*—and was served, and ate, a dainty appetizer of pineapple and cream cheese before she caught on.

Thus trapped—"I couldn't very well eat their food and then just get up and leave, could I?" she said—she stayed until the room was darkened for a slide presentation and then raced for a telephone to call, first, the flower show committee, and then Louis and me, to be sure we were all right.

As it happened, my father had stopped home between appointments, was already surprised to find Mother gone ("Not much of a gadabout"), and even more surprised to answer the telephone and learn that she was in Concord.

"What are you doing in Concord?" he asked.

Of course Mother was surprised too. She didn't expect my father to answer the phone and, caught unawares, had no ready reply. Once again, she had followed a strange car to an unknown destination, felt a little foolish and didn't want to go into it over the phone or, indeed, at all. No doubt she reasoned that what worked before would work again and said, "I don't know—but I'm coming straight home to fix the fish."

The idea here, a spur-of-the-moment notion, was to get his mind off one thing (her whereabouts) and onto something else (supper); and she thought the fish would do it, fish being his favorite meal.

It had no such effect. Had she gone to Concord to buy fish? he wondered. That made no sense, with a perfectly good fish market not ten minutes away. And even supposing there were better fish, or cheaper fish, or bigger fish in Concord, why hadn't she said so?

Louis and I were not only no help to him, but added fuel to the fire.

"When you left for school this morning," he asked us, "did your mother say she would be gone for the day?"

We said no.

"Well, was she dressed to go out?"

"I don't think so," Louis said. "She was in the kitchen, making meat loaf."

"For supper?"

He shrugged. "I guess so."

The meat loaf proved to be in the refrigerator with strips of bacon across the top of it, clearly ready for the oven—and in light of this, Mother's telephone conversation seemed not just strange and disjointed, but downright loony.

As my father later said, it was now clear to him that from time to time—indeed, *frequently*—something came over Mother; she would get in the car and drive somewhere (Fredonia, Concord) and then come to her senses and, exactly as she had told him, not know why she was wherever she was. The reference to fish struck him as an attempt on her part to hang onto reality: home, family, routine household matters.

It was at this point that he told Louis and me that Mother was not well, for he pictured a rocky time ahead and wanted to prepare us. He also planned to sit down quietly with Mother and try to talk about it—but then Mother came home with an enormous fish, complete with head and tail, opened the refrigerator and said, "Why, here's a meat loaf!"

She had forgotten about the meat loaf in all the confusion of the day, but her tone and choice of words suggested that she had never known anything about it in the first place. This convinced my father that she was in worse shape than he thought and needed more help than he could provide.

From here on, events marched off in all directions.

My father consulted Dr. Hildebrand, who said that Mother was the last person alive he would expect to go off her rocker; that if she had, it was out of his line; but that he would set up an appointment with her for a regular checkup and see what he could conclude.

He subsequently reported that Mother appeared

to him to be perfectly sane, though overconcerned about her sister Rhoda, and that to satisfy Mother, he had set up an appointment for Rhoda.

Following that consultation he told my father that if anyone had a problem it was Rhoda. "She's got pregnancy on the brain," he said. "Doesn't want to talk about diet and blood pressure. Wants to talk about babies; who has 'em, who wants 'em. I don't know"—he shook his head—"have to keep an eye on her."

Still, my father was not encouraged. Mother appeared to him to be perfectly sane, too, most of the time—but what about her amnesia jaunts to Fredonia and Concord? What about the meat loaf and the fish?

Meanwhile Louis and I were still waiting to be told about the baby, and Aunt Rhoda continued to come and go, waiting for Mother to break down and reveal whatever was troubling her and making her do the strange things my father said she did, and Mother went right on scrambling around the countryside from one flower show to another.

After the luncheon-lecture incident she was extremely cautious about following cars; but, as she later said, this system had worked for her more times than it hadn't. . . . When she next found herself heading into strange country with sketchy directions *(Trn rt at chkn frm; tke scd rt Briley?*

Borly?) she looked around for something likely . . . and found it, in a car whose rear window was literally abloom with pink and white blossoms.

She couldn't see the driver or the passengers, but neither had she seen anything along the road that might be a "chkn frm" and time was ticking by; so when this car turned off the highway she followed it.

The first thing that met her eye was a large billboard advertising Brown-Broast Broilers, which she took to be the Briley or Borly of her directions; and so she proceeded, confident and pleased with herself, until the flowery car stopped in front of the bank, and out stepped my father.

She had already pulled in behind him and there was no escape; but at least, as she said, this time the shoe was on the other foot. What was he doing in somebody else's car full of flowers? she demanded. And what was he doing here in Albion?

First of all, my father told her (gently, he later insisted), they weren't in Albion, but in Conneaut; he was here to make a business call; he was driving George Colgate's car because George asked him to; the flowers were all petunia plants to be delivered to George Colgate's mother-in-law, who lived in Conneaut.

"That is the craziest tale I ever heard!" Mother told him. She was, once again, upset with herself; exasperated with a driver who had led her astray; astonished that that driver should be my father; sick and tired of being late to flower shows; and fed up with the whole thing. "I'm supposed to be in Albion this very minute, judging a flower show. But because I followed you, I'm a long way from there."

"But why did you follow me?" my father asked.

"I thought you were going to the flower show."

"Why would I be going to a flower show, for God's sake?"

"Well, I didn't know it was *you*!"

And so it all came out—right there in front of the Citizens' Bank of Conneaut, before what my father called a cast of thousands.

"Let me try to understand this," he said. "Do you mean to tell me that for weeks you have been following just any old car, hoping it will lead you to where you want to go?"

"Not just any old car!" Mother said. "Do you think I'm crazy?"

Since that was exactly what he had thought, he said so, in the heat of the moment . . . and so all *that* came out—the consultation with Dr. Hildebrand; Rhoda's reason for being underfoot all the time; even the cautions to Louis and me—and it made Mother so furious that she got back in her car, slammed the door and drove away in a screech of tires.

By evening, though, they had both simmered down. They began to see the humor of the situation and produced appropriate peace offerings: My father brought a pot of the petunias home and set it in the middle of the table, like a flower show exhibit, and Mother presented him with a large baked haddock for dinner. They even became a little slaphappy, recalling to each other significant steps along the way: "You kept saying, I don't know why I'm here." "I just forgot about the meat loaf." Louis and I, encouraged by the convivial atmosphere, picked this time to say that we knew all about the baby, were very happy about it, and wanted to know when it was due.

My father, recalling his conversation with Dr. Hildebrand, instantly connected "baby" with Aunt Rhoda, assumed that Mother knew all about it and said, "I don't know. Grace, when is the baby due?"

Mother said, "Baby? What baby?" and my father said, "Why, Rhoda's baby"—which was, of course a big surprise to Louis and me.

Mother, though a little miffed that she was last in line to know this news, was overjoyed at the prospect of a new baby in the family. The very next day she dragged the crib and the buggy and the playpen out of the attic and hauled everything over to Aunt Rhoda, who, though fearful that Mother had finally slipped over the brink, nevertheless declared categorically that she, Rhoda, wasn't going to have any baby.

"Oh, yes, you are too," Mother said happily, hugging her. "And I should have guessed, because I was that very same way with Louis—nervous and a little blue, not quite myself, wondering whether I was too old . . ."

"What very same way?" Rhoda bristled. "I'm not nervous or blue and you're the one who's not quite herself!"

Mother said that was just a little misunderstanding, and she didn't want to talk about it, she'd rather talk about the baby.

"There *is* no baby!" Rhoda insisted.

"Then why did you say there was?" It suddenly occurred to Mother that she had been right all along about Rhoda, and she immediately adjusted her voice and manner to one of solicitous concern, saying things like "Don't get all excited" and "If you don't want to talk about it, we won't talk about it."

"Now, just stop that," Rhoda said. "I'm not crazy—you're the one who's supposed to be crazy!"

At this point a neighbor, attracted by the noise, stuck her head out a window, saw the pile of baby equipment and caught disjointed, but arresting, scraps of the conversation. And of course this news, such as it was—either my mother or Aunt Rhoda or both were either pregnant or crazy or both—spread through the neighborhood with the speed and spark of electricity and kept everyone alert and interested for a long time.

Mother refused to be embarrassed. She said it really didn't have anything to do with her . . . that she had simply been the calm center around which all the high winds blew. Aunt Rhoda was pretty mad, but eventually she cooled off too. My father said it was a good lesson for Louis and me.

"What did you learn from all this?" he asked.

I hadn't really learned anything except that Mother wasn't crazy, which had never occurred to me in the first place, but I knew that wasn't the right answer.

"Louis?" My father looked at him. "What do you have to say?"

Louis was ready. "Oh, what a tangled web we weave . . ." he said.

My father was absolutely delighted, but I was pretty sure that Louis didn't know what he was talking about, and I was right.

"What did I say?" he asked me later. "Dad loved it."

"It was exactly right," I told him. "It meant that if you tell lies, or don't tell the truth, or make things up, you'll get in a big mess. That was the lesson."

He frowned. "What about the other one?"

"There wasn't any other lesson, Louis."

"Sure, there was."

I could see that he meant it, that in all the confusion he had found some scrap of wisdom.

"If you're lost," he said, "find someone who isn't, and follow them."

The Adoption of Albert

There were so many children in our neighborhood that my mother was never surprised to find unfamiliar ones in the house, or in the backyard, or in my room, or in Louis's room.

"Well, who's this?" she would say, and she would then go on to connect that child with whatever house or family he belonged to.

But when Louis showed up with his new friend Albert, Mother had other things on her mind: the family reunion, which was two days away; the distant cousin who would be staying at our house; most of all, my Aunt Rhoda's famous Family Reunion cake, which, in Aunt Rhoda's absence, Mother felt obliged to provide.

Aunt Rhoda's absence, and the reason for it, were both first-time events: She had never before missed a family reunion, and neither she nor anyone else had ever before been called into court to testify about anything. Aunt Rhoda was to testify about an automobile accident she had witnessed—the only automobile accident in local memory, my father said, that did not involve Aunt Mildred.

All in all, it was a complicated time for Mother—cake, cousins, company—and when Louis appeared at the kitchen door and said, "This is Albert," she was too distracted to ask her usual questions.

Nor did she ask them at suppertime. By then she was up to her elbows in cake batter and left the three of us to eat alone with my father, who also didn't know Albert, but assumed that everyone else did.

I didn't know Albert either, but there was no reason why I should. He was Louis's friend, he was Louis's age, he even looked a lot like Louis—small and quiet and solemn—and it didn't occur to me to find out any more about him. I did ask, "Where do you live, Albert?"; and when he said, "Here," I just thought he meant here in the neighborhood instead of someplace else.

Mother thought the same thing. "Where does that little boy live?" she asked me the next morning, and I said, "Here," and she said, "I wonder which house?"

Albert had spent the night, and there was a note propped against the cereal box: *Albert and I have gone to dig worms.*

Louis had been collecting worms all summer and measuring them to see how long a worm got to be before it died. "I think that's what kills them," he said. "I think they die of length."

So far his longest worm was between four inches and four and a half inches. All his worms were between one size and another because they wouldn't hold still. "It's really hard," he said. "I have to stretch them out and measure them at the same time, and if I'm not careful they come apart."

"Oh, Louis," I said, "that's awful! What do you do then?"

He shrugged. "I bury the pieces. What else can I do?"

Of course, most kids wouldn't even do that, but Louis was neater than most kids.

It was late afternoon when he and Albert came back, and they had big news. They also had two coffee cans full of worm parts.

"I thought you buried them," I said.

"I didn't have to! Albert says . . . Albert

says . . ." I had never seen Louis so pleased and excited. "Tell her what you said."

"It doesn't kill them," Albert said. "The tail ends grow new heads, and the head ends grow new tails."

I looked in the coffee cans, but I couldn't tell the difference between head and tails. Louis said he couldn't tell the difference either. "But it doesn't matter," he said, "because the worms can. *They* know. We're going to keep them, and watch them grow, and measure them . . . and maybe name them."

"They're no trouble," Albert said. "They just eat dirt. We've got some." He held up another coffee can.

They took all three coffee cans up to Louis's room, and this worried me a lot because I knew I would have to sleep in Louis's room when everybody came for the family reunion.

My father said he was always astonished that there was anybody left to *come* to the family reunion. "Your whole family is already here," he told Mother, "living around the corner, or three streets away, or on the other side of town."

"Not everybody," Mother said. "There's Virginia and Evelyn and Clyde . . ." She reeled off the names—cousins, mostly, whom we knew only from Christmas cards, and from their annual appearance at the reunion.

Some, in fact, had already appeared and were upstairs unpacking their suitcases. Mother, who was busy catching up on their news and shuffling food around in the refrigerator and getting out all the dishes and silverware, either didn't realize that Albert was still with us or just didn't remember that she had ever seen him in the first place.

My father had gone off to borrow picnic tables for the next day, and since I didn't want to sit around and watch worms grow, I went next door to play with my friend Maxine Slocum and forgot all about Albert.

That night when I took my sleeping bag into Louis's room, he was already asleep in a mound of bedclothes . . . and there was another mound of bedclothes beside him.

"Louis." I shook him awake. "Who is that?"

"It's Albert," he said.

"Why doesn't he go home?"

Louis looked surprised. "He *is* home. He's going to live here now. Remember? He told you. . . . Don't worry, Mary Elizabeth," he added. "You'll like Albert."

"I already like Albert," I said, "but I don't think he can live here. I think he has to live with his parents."

"He doesn't want to," Louis said. "He even told

them so. He told them, 'I don't want to live with you anymore,' and they said, 'All right, Albert, you just go and live someplace else.' "

I had never heard of such a thing, except when my friend Wanda McCall baptized the hamsters with her mother's French perfume. The house smelled wonderful, but all the hamsters got sick and so did Mrs. McCall, and Mr. McCall gave Wanda two dollars and told her to get lost. But he didn't mean forever.

Neither had Albert's parents, I decided. They would probably call tomorrow and tell him to come home.

"Louis." I shook him again. "Where are the worms?"

"They aren't worms yet," he reminded me. "The cans are in the closet."

I didn't think either half of a worm could go very far, but I put my sleeping bag on the other side of the room anyway, just in case.

When I woke up the next morning Louis and Albert were gone, but they had made the bed and folded up their clothes and left a note that said, *We'll be back for the picnic. Please don't move the worms.* There was a P.S.: *Tell the lady cousin in the purple underwear that I'm sorry. I didn't know she was in there.* Then there was another P.S.: *It was really Albert, but pretend it was me and tell her I'm sorry. Or if you don't want to, just find out who she is and I'll tell her.*

That was nice of Louis, I thought, but I really didn't want to ask around about everyone's underwear.

"I guess not," Louis said later. "It's okay . . . Albert felt bad about it, that's all."

"Where is Albert?" I asked.

"Over there." Louis pointed to where Mother's brother Frank was taking pictures with his new Polaroid camera.

"You'll have to get closer together," we heard him say, "and put Clyde's boy in front of you, Blanche."

"Who is Clyde's boy?" Louis asked me.

"I think it's Albert," I said. "He's the only boy there."

I was right. "Looks just *like* Clyde," we heard Aunt Blanche say.

I thought Albert looked a little worried, but Louis said he was just worried about the worms. "We're going to move them someplace else," he said. "Albert thinks they might get out and crawl around—especially the head parts, Albert said, because they could see where they were going."

That made me shiver, so I hoped they would put them somewhere up high.

By then Aunt Rhoda had arrived, to everyone's

surprise. She never did get to testify, she said, because "the litigants" had to go to the police station to look at "mug shots" and "supply ID's." Aunt Rhoda had picked up a whole new vocabulary.

"Mug shots?" my father said. "ID's? Now, what does that mean? This was a traffic accident, not a holdup."

"I don't know," Mother told him. "Rhoda just said they had to study mug shots of children."

"There is no such thing as mug shots of children. Mug shots are of criminals. Rhoda's got it all wrong." He went to question Aunt Rhoda further and stumbled into the one event he always tried to avoid: the big family photograph, with everyone in it.

Uncle Frank had set up a different camera and lined everybody up, but he was missing some people: my parents, Aunt Mildred . . . "And Louis," he said. "And Clyde's boy. Clyde, where's your boy?"

Clyde looked surprised. "He's in the Army."

"I mean the little one."

"Looks just like you," Aunt Blanche put in.

"He doesn't look one bit like me," Clyde said. "He looks like his mother."

"No," Aunt Blanche said stubbornly. "He looks like you."

Clyde was stubborn too. "How do you know

what he looks like, Blanche? You haven't seen him in six years!"

"I saw him fifteen minutes ago!"

"Who?" my father said, arriving on the scene with Mother.

"They're talking about Albert," I said. "Louis's friend Albert."

"Albert!" Mother looked amazed. "Is that little boy here again?"

"He never left," I said.

So I was sent to get Albert, and find out where he lived, while Mother explained to everybody who he was (which was hard, because she didn't *know* who he was), and my father pressed Aunt Rhoda for more details about her experiences in court—fearful, he later said, that she had wandered into the wrong courtroom and the wrong trial, and was now mixed up with a bunch of criminals.

I found Louis crawling around the floor of his room. "We dropped some of a worm," he said, "but only one, and I'll find it. We took the rest of them out of the closet."

"Mother wants to know where Albert lives," I told him.

"You mean . . . besides here?" Louis was being stubborn too, just like Aunt Blanche and Clyde. "I don't know."

"Well, what's Albert's name?"

"You mean . . . besides Albert? I'll ask him."

"But, Louis—don't you know?"

"I only met him day before yesterday," Louis said. "He was sitting on the curb outside the model-airplane store, after his parents told him to go live someplace else. He didn't know anyplace else, so I told him he could live here. And after that, all we talked about was worms."

Albert didn't know where he lived either. "I can't remember," he said. "We haven't lived there long enough for me to remember. I think it's the name of a tree."

Albert was right. He lived on Catalpa Street, and his name was Henderson. But it was Aunt Rhoda, of all people, who supplied the information, while Louis and Albert were upstairs looking for the missing worm.

Aunt Rhoda recognized Albert in the Polaroid picture because, when she witnessed the automobile accident, she had also witnessed Albert in one of the cars with his parents—the very same people, she said, who were at this moment examining mug shots at the police station.

"Isn't it a small world!" Aunt Rhoda said . . . and everyone agreed, except my father.

He had assumed, all along, that Mother knew who Albert was and knew where Albert came from. "And I suppose," he said, "that Albert is staying with us now because his parents have to be in court—but didn't the Hendersons mention *why* they had to be in court?"

"I don't know the Hendersons," Mother said.

"Well, did Albert . . ."

"I don't know Albert either." Mother was getting testy under all this cross-examination. "Obviously, Louis said it would be all right for Albert to stay here—and it *is* all right," she said. "Those poor people have enough trouble. That's the least we can do for them."

In the meantime Louis and Albert came downstairs—"We found the worm," Louis assured me—went to get more fried chicken and potato salad, and ran into Aunt Rhoda, who said she was certainly surprised to see Albert again and to see him *here.*

"I live here," Albert said.

"Oh, no," Aunt Rhoda laughed. "You live on Catalpa Street."

"Not anymore," Albert said.

Of course Aunt Rhoda reported this to Mother, who was by then completely mystified about Albert, and pretty fed up with all the sketchy bits and pieces of news about him. She left Aunt Rhoda to cut the Family Reunion cake and make the coffee, and went off to find Louis. My father, having also concluded that Louis was the key to it all, had done the same thing.

Between them, they quickly figured out that

Louis did not know the Hendersons and that he barely knew Albert . . . and that Albert had left home and was prepared to live with us forever.

My father called the police station, where the Hendersons were indeed studying pictures of missing children and supplying information about their own missing child . . . and in no time they arrived at our house and were reunited with Albert.

This was exactly the kind of happy ending my mother loved best—even Albert seemed happy to be back with his family.

"Well, now he has a friend," Mrs. Henderson said, beaming at Louis. "That was the trouble. He didn't know anyone, didn't have anyone to play with or talk to. Thank goodness for you, Louis!"

The Hendersons obviously saw Louis as the hero of it all, which exasperated my father.

"I don't know why you're so grumpy," Mother said. "Just suppose Louis hadn't come along and found Albert outside the airplane store—then what?"

"Then Albert would have gone home where he belonged," my father said, "and none of this would have happened."

"Exactly!" Mother said. "And he would still be a lonely, unhappy little boy . . . way over there on Catalpa Street."

She invited the Hendersons to stay for cake and coffee, and to meet all the relatives. Aunt Rhoda said she couldn't meet them officially, or talk to them, because of being a witness, but she waved to them from the back porch, and Mrs. Henderson waved back and called to her, "Your cake recipe is wonderful!"

"Have some coffee," Mother said. "It's Rhoda's coffee, too."

Aunt Rhoda said later that it was pretty silly to call it *her* coffee just because she'd made it, and she also said that she didn't feel one bit responsible for what had happened.

"In my house," she said, "if a can says coffee, that's what's in it, and it wouldn't occur to me to look."

Mother said, in all fairness, it wouldn't occur to her to look either. . . . "Except, of course, I don't keep my coffee on that high shelf, so I might have looked."

My father, who had been the first one to sip the coffee—and, therefore, the *only* one to sip the coffee—said he wished *someone* had looked.

"Was it the can full of dirt?" I asked Louis, and he shook his head no.

"Oh, I'm sorry, Louis," I said, "but you and Albert can get some more worms."

"And it was only the tail ends, anyway," Albert said . . . although I hadn't really wanted to know that.

Marcella and Me

Until he was seven years old, Louis thought he would eventually catch up with me, and we would be the same age.

"Then what?" I asked. "Would we be the same age forever?"

"Wouldn't you like to?" Louis said. "We could be seventeen."

Like most of Louis's ideas, this one was wonderful but weird. "Sure I'd like to, Louis," I said, "but it won't work. I'm always going to be older than you are. I'll be seventeen before you are and then I'll have to go on and be eighteen, and you will, too. We can't do anything about it."

He was looking stubborn, so I said, "Believe me, Louis. It's like being *who* you are. We can't do anything about that either."

"I don't want to do anything about that," he said. "So far, I *like* that, don't you?"

Louis never changed his mind about being who he was, but I had to change my mind in a hurry when Aunt Rhoda joined the local Historical Society and began to trace the family's background.

Until then, no one even knew there *was* a local Historical Society, and my father said he would like to keep it that way. "You have enough family around right now," he told Mother, "without Rhoda digging up all the ones who *used* to be around."

Louis's eyes got wide. "She's going to dig them up?" he said. "Can you do that?"

"Not the actual people," Mother told him. "She's going to look up everyone's records: births and deaths and marriages, things like that. I think it's wonderful of Rhoda to do this. Now you and Mary Elizabeth will know who all your ancestors were, right back to the beginning."

Louis thought the beginning would be George Washington, but my father said not to count on it. He also said that Aunt Rhoda might get some surprises.

The first surprise turned out to be the biggest.

"Rhoda has found a whole new person in the family," Mother reported. "Someone we never knew anything about." She had no further details, because, she said, Rhoda was very mysterious about the whole thing and wanted to tell us in person. But when Aunt Rhoda arrived that evening she refused to tell anybody anything until Louis and I left the room.

"But it's their family too," Mother said, and Aunt Rhoda raised her eyebrows and nodded her head up and down very fast.

We left the room, but as soon as Aunt Rhoda passed on her news my father made so much noise about it that we heard everything anyway, so we went back in.

"Our baby!?!" we heard him say, his voice rising. "What baby? We don't have any more babies, you know that. What's wrong with you, Rhoda?"

Aunt Rhoda said there wasn't anything wrong with her now, but she had nearly passed out from shock when she found this birth certificate. " 'Marcella Lawson,' " she read aloud. " 'Parents, Fred and Grace Lawson.' "

Louis poked me. "That's us," he said, "but who's Marcella? Do we have a sister? Where is she?"

"I don't know," I said. Where, indeed? Hidden away someplace? Given away to somebody?

"It must be some other Fred and Grace Lawson," Mother suggested, but Aunt Rhoda said that would be pretty unusual in such a small town; and, anyway, they weren't in the phone book.

"Maybe they moved away," my father said. He looked at the birth certificate. "This was eleven years ago . . . eleven years next month. They had this baby, and then they moved away."

"What day next month?" Mother looked at the birth certificate too. "Well, what do you know about that? We must have been in the hospital together, because that's Mary Elizabeth's birthday, and she'll be eleven."

Louis poked me again. "You're twins," he said.

"And what's more," Mother went on, "we have a second cousin named Marcella—Marcella Potter."

"But it couldn't be her," Aunt Rhoda said. "She lives way out in Denver, Colorado."

My father stared at both of them. "Of course it's not her! She doesn't have anything to do with this."

"I know she doesn't," Mother said, "but it *is* a coincidence, because she's the only Marcella in the family. She told me that once, in a letter, and she said why didn't I name a baby after her, and then there'd be another Marcella."

There was a long silence.

"Well, I didn't *do* it!" Mother said, but she didn't sound too sure, and there was another long silence, while everybody looked at the birth certificate, and at Mother, and at me.

"Apparently that's just what you did," my father

said finally. "You must have been half asleep from the anesthetic, and they came and said, 'What's this baby's name?' and you said, 'The baby's name is Marcella.' "

At first mother refused to believe that she had done such a thing, and then she refused to believe that it made any difference anyway. . . . "Everybody knows who Mary Elizabeth is."

My father said that wasn't the point. "Someday, somewhere, Mary Elizabeth is going to have to produce a birth certificate to prove that she is who she says she is, and *this* birth certificate"—he waved it in the air—"just proves that she isn't."

I must have looked worried, because Louis said, "Just tell them you don't have one. Say it got burned up in a fire."

That sounded good to me, but I was pretty sure it wouldn't satisfy the authorities, and in the meantime . . . who *was* I?

"I think you have to be Marcella," Louis said. "I think it's the law."

I thought so too. We were both scared of the law and anxious not to break it, and we were both impressed by the birth certificate, which looked too important to ignore.

I didn't get much chance to be Marcella, though, because Mother was right about one thing—everybody already knew who I was. What I needed was a lot of perfect strangers who would ask, "What is your name, little girl?" so I could say "Marcella Lawson" over and over again, till it sounded natural.

"You should ride the bus to Chillicothe and get lost," Louis said. "When you're lost, everyone wants to know who you are, and you have to say your name about a million times."

This was a good idea, but I didn't have any money to ride the bus to Chillicothe. Mother had promised us a nickel apiece for every Japanese beetle we picked off her rosebushes; but I couldn't bear to touch them and Louis couldn't bear to drop them into the can of kerosene, so between us we only captured four and only collected twenty cents. Chillicothe was out.

Whenever Louis thought about it, *he* would call me Marcella; but he didn't think about it very often, and when he did, I never remembered who he was talking to.

Neither did anyone else. My father never said, "Good for you, Louis. She'd better get used to Marcella, because that's going to be her name forever." My mother didn't call up all her friends and relations to tell them who I was now, and when the new Avon lady said, "Is this your daughter, Mrs. Lawson?" Mother said, "Yes, this is my daughter, Mary Elizabeth."

This was very puzzling to Louis and me, but, as we eventually learned, my father had taken the birth certificate back to the Town Clerk right away, explained the situation, had it corrected and put the whole thing out of his mind—while Mother had managed to convince herself that it was all somebody's else foolish mistake—the hospital, the town clerk, maybe even Aunt Rhoda—and put the whole thing out of her mind, too. Consequently, there was no one to help me remember who I was except Louis, who was willing but unreliable.

"Listen, Louis," I said finally, "this is too complicated. I'm just going to be Mary Elizabeth."

Louis frowned and began to shake his head, and I knew he was thinking about the birth certificate, with its big official seal and all the signatures that said *WITNESS* in fancy writing, so I said, "I know my *real* name is Marcella, and I have to be Marcella if I do anything that's legal. But I won't have to do anything legal till I'm all grown up . . . except say the pledge of allegiance, and you don't have to say your name for that." I knew that Louis *did* say his name: "I, Louis, pledge allegiance . . ."; but that was just his own idea.

Like Mother, I put the whole thing out of my mind, too; and when, a few days later, a package arrived for my father—"Have to sign for it," the delivery man said. "Insured freight, special delivery—sign right there"—I signed the only name I'd lived with for eleven years.

"Okay, that makes it legal," the man said. "It's your responsibility." He looked at my signature. " 'Mary Elizabeth Lawson'—right?" And he was gone before I could do anything.

"But what *could* I do?" I asked Louis. "I couldn't say, 'Wait a minute, that's not my real name.' He would have taken away the package . . . and, Louis, look at the package."

It was a big, long, heavy package, plastered all over with *SPECIAL DELIVERY* stickers, and *THIS END UP* stickers. It looked important and expensive—and most of all, legal.

My father was delighted. He had been waiting for it, he said, and he turned to my mother with a big smile on his face. "It's for you," he said. "It's just what you want."

Mother looked puzzled. "It can't be. It isn't big enough."

"It's the biggest size they make."

"The biggest refrigerator?"

My father stared. "It isn't a *refrigerator*! I didn't know you wanted a refrigerator."

Actually, Mother had not yet mentioned that she wanted a refrigerator, and she had been briefly (*very* briefly) surprised and pleased that he would have guessed this. She was also sorry to have spoiled his pleasure about the unexpected present, and she prepared herself to be crazy about it, whatever it was.

It was a big, round, ugly lamp on top of a long straight pole, and Mother said immediately, "Oh, you're right. I just love it. Where will we put it?"

"You don't even know what it is yet," my father said, "but you *will* love it. It goes outside. It's a Beetle Eater."

He set it in the yard beside Mother's rosebushes and plugged it in, while we all watched and waited.

Slowly the lamp began to revolve and to glow with a dark-orange light and to make a high, thin, screechy noise . . . and then, before our very eyes, Japanese beetles, by twos and threes, whirred away from the rosebushes and into the Beetle Eater and killed themselves.

It worked perfectly—the next morning there were four inches of dead beetles piled up inside the lamp—but Mother said she couldn't stand it.

"You can't stand the noise?" my father said. "The orange light bothers you? . . . What?"

"It's the beetles," Mother said. "All those dead beetles."

"But you drop them into kerosene!"

"It's not the same thing," Mother said. "If you're a beetle, you have to expect that."

This must have sounded as crazy to Mother as it did to the rest of us, because she went on, "I just mean, that's what happens to beetles. In a way, it's natural. But it's not natural to lure them into an orange lamp and burn them crispy."

She refused to change her mind, and my father said he wasn't going to spend thirty-four dollars and ninety-five cents for a Beetle Eater if we weren't going to let it eat beetles. "I'll send it back," he said. "I still have the receipt."

Louis and I looked at each other. I had signed the receipt, with my illegal name.

"You can't let him send it back," Louis said. "They'll come after you. Like Dad said, you'll have to prove who you are, and you can't."

"Louis," I said, "I'm only eleven years old. What can they do to me?"

"They can make you pay for the Beetle Eater."

"But we've already got the Beetle Eater."

"Not if Dad sends it back," he said.

"Of course I'm going to send it back," my father told me. "That's a lot of money. Thirty-four dollars and ninety-five cents is worth a fight." I must have looked alarmed, because he went on. "Well, they won't *want* to take it back. I can't very well say it didn't work, and I refuse to say that your mother feels sorry for the beetles. I'm just going to have to return it and say, here it is. And they won't like that. So"—he picked up his newspaper—"there'll be a fight about it."

This was the worst news yet. I pictured somebody pounding on a table and yelling, "Get hold of whoever signed for it!"; so I said the first thing that came to mind.

"Please don't send it back. Give it to me—for my birthday."

My father stared at me. "Why?"

I couldn't think of any reason why I would want a Beetle Eater: I didn't like beetles, dead or alive; I didn't like loud screechy noises; and I'd already said the orange light hurt my eyes. "I just want it. Please. You don't have to give me anything else."

I suppose my father, however bewildered by my request, saw in this an opportunity to avoid both a fight with the Beetle Eater company and a struggle with packing crates and wrapping paper—and Mother, despite her objections to *this* contraption, understood that people do, often, simply want an unlikely thing for no good reason except that they want it. She had once wanted, had bought and then stuck away in the attic a very large framed picture of dogs playing poker—and whenever she cleaned the attic she would say, of this picture, "I don't know why I wanted it so much. I just did."

Luckily, no one held me to my bargain, and I did get some other presents, including a package addressed, mysteriously, to *Grace Lawson and Daughter.*

"I don't know what it is," Mother said, "and I can't even read the postmark. But it does say daughter, and it's your birthday, so you open it."

It was a baby bonnet and a pair of pink booties

and the card said, *For my namesake.* It was signed *Cousin Marcella.*

When confronted with this evidence, Aunt Rhoda admitted that she had, in fact, mentioned Mother's mistake to Cousin Marcella Potter.

"I wrote to her for some information about the family background, and then I just said, *P.S. Did you know that Grace named a baby after you, by accident?* I *think* I said, by accident." She looked at the booties. "Obviously she got it all wrong."

I wondered whether I would have to write Cousin Marcella a thank-you letter, and what I would say in it. We weren't supposed to just say, *Thank you for the present.* We were supposed to say something *about* the present, and I didn't know what to say about the pink booties.

"Nothing," my father said. "You're off the hook. This woman thinks you're a new baby. And anyway," he added, "she sent the booties to her namesake, but she hasn't got one, because I had your birth certificate changed."

I was very relieved to hear this, because it felt peculiar to be somebody else, even secretly. As far as I was concerned, Marcella *was* somebody else (maybe somebody who could recite all fifty states, and do long division without a mistake and tap-dance) but even so, like Louis, I was satisfied to be me. I was sorry, though, that I had pleaded for the Beetle Eater instead of something equally expensive and more desirable, like my own telephone.

I assumed that the Beetle Eater would end up in the attic, along with the bonnet and the booties and the dog picture, but Louis and his friend Albert plugged it in one night after beetle season was over; and in the still, clear night air, it caused a sensation in the neighborhood. Two people called the newspaper to report a strange orange light and a weird unearthly sound in our backyard, and the next day there was an article on the front page:

OUTER SPACE ALIEN?
VISITS LOCAL FAMILY.

For two or three days there was a steady stream of cars driving past our house, and a parade of kids perfectly willing to pay a dime to see the outer space alien perform . . . and Louis and I made $4.60 before the orange light burned out and the noise died down and the first snow fell on the Beetle Eater.

Vergil, the Laid-back Dog

Most of Mother's relatives had animals of one kind or another, and most of the animals, according to my father, were as strange as the people they belonged to.

"I don't know," he often said, "whether they actively seek out screwy dogs and cats, or whether the dogs and cats just turn screwy after a while." He included our cat Leroy in this overall opinion, although by then Leroy was gone. He/she had produced four kittens and immediately took off for greener pastures, abandoning both us and the kittens, which my father said was completely unnatural behavior, and proved his point.

Actually there were any number of perfectly ordinary pets in the family—faithful nondescript dogs, companionable cats—but, just as good news is less dramatic than bad news and therefore less publicized, these humdrum animals were never the ones my father heard about, and the ones he *did* hear about left him forever cool to the idea of having one of his own.

Mother knew this; but, as she later said, having a dog was one thing, and having a dog come to visit for a few days was something else. So when her cousin Lloyd Otway deposited his dog Vergil on our doorstep, Mother didn't think twice about offering to keep Vergil while Lloyd went off to Milwaukee, Wisconsin, to acquire a wife.

My father said he could understand that Lloyd might find the pickings slim and overfamiliar right here at home, "—but why take off for Milwaukee?"

"Because that's where Pauline lives," Mother said. "Pauline Swavel. That's where she went back to after she and Lloyd met and fell in love. Oh, Fred, you remember Pauline!"

Obviously he didn't; but in view of the romantic circumstances involving Lloyd and Pauline Swavel, I did; and I remembered, too, that my father had been out of town that day.

"That's right, he was," Mother said. "He was in Columbus. You were in Columbus that day, at your state convention. I know I told you about it, but you probably didn't hear me, or else you didn't listen."

"That *day*?!?" My father stared at her. "Lloyd and this Pauline met and fell in love in one day?"

"Yes," Mother said—and this was, indeed, the case: a one-day, whirlwind, love-at-first-sight affair, attended by the usual monkey puzzle of mistakes and coincidences.

Pauline Swavel, while driving through town on her way from West Virginia, was run into by Aunt Mildred, who had been distracted by the unexpected appearance in her car of Lloyd's dog Vergil.

"All of a sudden, there he was," she said. "Don't know where he came from. Just sat up in the backseat and yawned and stretched and groaned—scared me to death, and I hit the gas instead of the brake."

Vergil, equally alarmed, began to leap up and down in the car and to scramble from back to front, howling and barking. This behavior was so unnatural in Vergil—who had, at various times, slept through a fire, a burglary, and an explosion at the fertilizer plant—that Aunt Mildred lost all control, careened through a traffic light and bounced off a milk truck and into Pauline, who had pulled over to study her road map.

Pauline had taken a wrong turn somewhere north of Parkersburg and was not only completely lost but, now, involved in a traffic accident as well—

with a car that seemed to her, at first glance, to be driven by a dog.

At this point Lloyd appeared. He had been delivering lawn fertilizer to Aunt Mildred, missed Vergil, and knew immediately what had happened, since it was Vergil's habit to climb into whatever car was handy and open and go to sleep.

Lloyd set out at once to find and follow Aunt Mildred—never an easy task, but a little easier this time because of all the commotion at the scene of the accident.

He arrived; retrieved Vergil; assessed the damage, which was minor; ignored Aunt Mildred (or so she said); and, on the spot, fell in love with Pauline. That Pauline should, at the very same moment, fall in love with Lloyd seemed insane to Aunt Mildred and my mother; unlikely to Louis—"Unless it was a movie," he said—and gloriously romantic to me.

"But, Lloyd," Mother said when he arrived at our house later that day, arm in arm with Pauline, to tell us the news, "isn't this awfully sudden?"

"Like a lightning bolt," Lloyd said.

"And, Pauline," Mother went on, "of course we think the world and all of Lloyd . . . but you don't even know him!"

"I feel I do," Pauline said, "after just these few hours. I've never felt so comfortable with a person, nor found anyone so easy to talk to. I figure that whatever I don't know about Lloyd, or what he doesn't know about me, will give us conversation for years. Do you believe in fate, Mrs. Lawson?"

"No, I don't," Mother said, "not when it's mixed up with Mildred and a bird dog."

"Neither do I," Pauline said, "or never did till now. But just think about it. . . . Why did I get lost and end up here? Why did Lloyd's dog get into someone else's car? Why did your sister run into me instead of someone else?"

Now, explaining it all to my father, Mother agreed that these were not mysterious events: Vergil was famous for getting into anybody's car, Aunt Mildred was famous for colliding with anybody's car, and . . . "I know all about getting lost," Mother said, "but even I know there are only two main roads north from Parkersburg, and if you miss the other one you'll end up here. But after all, they're both grown-up people—Lloyd's thirty-three years old, it's time he got married—and it wasn't as if they were going to get married that very minute. Besides, I thought it would all fizzle out. Of course, it didn't"—she smiled happily—"and now Lloyd's gone off to Milwaukee to marry Pauline."

My father eyed Vergil. "I think if I were Lloyd," he said, "I'd take that dog along with me for good luck, since he was in on the beginning of this romance."

"Well, so was Mildred," Mother said, "but she

can't just go off to Milwaukee either—and you don't fool me a bit. You just don't want Vergil underfoot."

Unfortunately, because of his large and rangy size, Vergil was automatically underfoot, and he usually chose to sprawl, full-length, in awkward places: at the top of the stairs or at the bottom of the stairs, under the dining-room table, under my father's car and, from time to time, on very warm days, in the bathtub.

The first time this happened Louis tried to make Vergil more comfortable by turning on the water; but Vergil scrambled out of the bathtub (moving faster than we had ever seen him move before) and tore all around the upstairs, barking and howling and shaking himself and spraying water everywhere.

"I think he was asleep," Louis said, "and it surprised him."

I thought so too, because Vergil was asleep most of the time . . . but when Louis tried it again, Vergil was awake and the same thing happened.

"He doesn't like the water," Mother said. "He just likes to feel the cool porcelain tub."

"So do I," my father said, "but I don't want to take turns with a big hairy dog. Isn't Lloyd back yet? He must be married by now."

"Yes," Mother said, "but they're on their honeymoon. Surely you don't begrudge them a honeymoon?"

"That depends on where they went," my father said. "They could have a very nice honeymoon between Milwaukee and here—two or three days in Chicago, maybe."

"Yes," Mother said, "they could. Listen, is that the telephone?"

"Well, hurry up and answer it. Maybe it's Lloyd."

It wasn't Lloyd. Actually, it wasn't even the telephone—Mother just made that up because she didn't want to explain that Lloyd and Pauline had gone in the opposite direction—to San Francisco—and were going to stop along the way wherever Pauline had relatives who wanted to welcome Lloyd into the family. We found out later that all these relatives lived in places like Middle Mine, Wyoming, and Clash, Nebraska, and were probably overjoyed to see anybody at all.

Of course, after two or three weeks, Mother had to admit that they weren't in Chicago and, as far as she knew, never had been. "They probably aren't even to San Francisco yet," she said. "You know how southerners are—sometimes newlywed couples visit around for months."

"But Pauline isn't a southerner, she's from Milwaukee!"

"I was just giving you an example," Mother said.

"It wouldn't have to be southerners. Amish people do the same thing."

"Is Pauline Amish?"

"She didn't say."

My father thought that over briefly and then shook his head. "You don't have any idea where they are, do you."

"No . . . but I do know that Lloyd is lucky, to marry into such a close and loving family."

"Lloyd is lucky," my father said, "because he was able to unload this dog on us while he tours the entire western half of the country. Oh, well," he sighed. "I'm going to take a bath—he isn't in the bathtub, is he?"

"No," Mother said, "but be careful when you come downstairs. He's asleep on the top step."

Three or four minutes later Louis and I heard the unmistakable *thump, thump, bang, thump, bang* of something or somebody falling downstairs, and went to see who or what it was.

My father heard the noise too, assumed that Mother had tripped over Vergil and came stumbling out of the bathroom with his pants half off, calling for us to get help. Mother, in the back bedroom, heard both the thumps and the cries for help, came running from that end of house and fell over my father, who was trapped by his pants.

Meanwhile, Vergil lay at the foot of the stairs in his customary position: full-length and flat on his back—and ominously still. We thought he might be dead, and Louis got down on the floor to listen to his heart . . . which led Mother to conclude that it was Louis who had fallen *over* Vergil and then down the stairs along *with* Vergil.

"What else would I think?" she said. "Everybody on the floor in a heap." She felt responsible, though, and made my father pull on his pants and take Vergil to the animal hospital, where, as it turned out, he was well known.

"He isn't moving," Mother said. "He fell down the stairs."

"Does it all the time," the doctor told us. "This is the laziest dog in the world. He'd *rather* fall down stairs than stand up. Fell off a shed roof once. Fell out of Lloyd's truck that was loaded with fertilizer bags."

"But he isn't moving," Mother said.

"That's because he's asleep."

My father said this was the last straw—that he hadn't wanted a dog at all, and he especially didn't want a dog who was too lazy to stand up—but Mother was relieved.

"I'd hate to have Lloyd come back," she said, "and have to tell him that his dog died of injuries."

"At this rate," my father said, "his dog will die of old age before he shows up."

Vergil didn't die, but Lloyd and Pauline never did show up, either. Their car broke down in a place called Faltrey, Arkansas . . . *and we couldn't find anyone to fix it,* Lloyd wrote. *They had a garage, had a gas station, had parts and equipment, had no mechanic. The mechanic couldn't stand Arkansas, they said, and he got on his motorcycle and left. So I fixed our car and two or three other people's cars . . . and to make a long story short, they just wouldn't let us leave. And now you couldn't pay us to leave, because we love it here in Faltrey, especially Pauline. But don't worry, because we'll be back to get Vergil, the first chance we get.*

" 'Yours truly, Lloyd,' " Mother finished reading. "Well, what do you know about that!"

"I know it's a long way to Arkansas," my father said, looking at Vergil.

After that we got a few postcards from Lloyd and a few letters from Pauline, who sent us a picture of the garage and a picture of their house and, eventually, a picture of their baby. All the cards and letters said they would be back for Vergil . . . *as soon as Lloyd's work lets up a little* or *as soon as we get the tomatoes in the garden* or *as soon as the baby's old enough to travel.*

My mother believed all these assurances (or said she did), and she would never admit that Vergil was anything but a temporary house guest. If anyone mentioned "your dog," she would always say, "Oh, this is Lloyd's dog. We're just keeping him for Lloyd."

In a way, my father wouldn't admit it either, because he never referred to Vergil as "our dog" or "my dog" or anything except "that dog"; but when Lloyd and Pauline finally did come back they had a sizeable family—Lloyd, Jr., was in the second grade, and the twin girls were two and a half years old—and their car was full of infant seats and baby beds and toys. My mother said the last thing they needed was Vergil. "Where would you put him?" she said.

Lloyd agreed. "I guess I just forgot how big he is. We'd better bring the truck next time."

Mother didn't mention this to my father, and in fact, Lloyd and Pauline had been gone for three days before he realized that Vergil didn't go with them, although Vergil was in plain sight, asleep, the whole time.

"You're just used to him," Mother said, "and you would miss him a lot."

"How could I possibly miss him if I haven't even noticed him for three days?"

"There!" she said. "How could any dog be less trouble!"

She was right, of course. Vergil didn't bark, or bite people, or dig up gardens, or upset trash cans, and by then we were all used to stepping over him or around him. By then, too, he was too old to climb into the bathtub; but sometimes, on very hot days, my father would lift him in—to get him out of the way, he said—and then get mad because Vergil wouldn't climb back out.

Despite Vergil's lack of interest in us, Louis and I were very fond of him. We thought of him as our dog, played with him during those brief and very occasional moments when he was awake, and whenever we had to write a paper for school about *My Best Friend*, or *My Favorite Pet*, we wrote about Vergil.

We never got very good grades on these papers because there was so little to tell, but we did share the glory when Vergil won a blue ribbon in the YMCA Pet Show. He won it for "Unusual Obedience to Command"—we commanded him to "play dead," and no dog did it better or for so long.

Misplaced Persons

Mother was not the only member of her family to be intimidated by automobiles, just as Aunt Mildred was not the only one to have exactly opposite feelings. In fact, they all seemed to be either one way or the other, with the exception of my little brother Louis, who enjoyed driving a car (till he was found out and stopped), but did so without risk to anyone's life or limbs.

The extreme cases were Aunt Mildred, with whom Louis and I were forbidden to ride—and, at the other end of the scale, Aunt Blanche. My father said that with Aunt Mildred we were apt to be killed outright, but with Aunt Blanche we would probably die of old age while waiting to turn left at an intersection.

When, on one occasion, circumstances required him to be her passenger, he said that he saw parts of town previously unknown to him as she drove blocks and blocks out of her way to avoid crossing traffic.

"I would tell her, 'You can turn here, Blanche,' " he said, "but she would never do it. We would go on three or four streets, turn right, turn right, turn right again. We were trying to get to the bank, and you could *see* the bank, but it might as well have been on the other side of a river. . . . Never again!"

Aunt Blanche's travels were further complicated by her poor sense of direction (a failing she shared with my mother), and by her insistence on beginning any trip, long or short, at the post office. Since she didn't live very far from the post office, it wasn't unusual for her to drive past it often, in the natural course of events . . . but even if she was headed for the other end of town in the opposite direction she still drove first to the post office and then took off from there.

This seemed odd but harmless, and no one paid much attention, though there were various opinions about the reason for it. Aunt Rhoda thought Aunt Blanche didn't want the mailman to know all her business, and to prevent this, just picked up her own mail. This was a sore point with Aunt Rhoda, since *her* mailman was notorious for reading postcards and return addresses and, on at least one occasion, for observing that Aunt Rhoda certainly did a lot of business with the Spencer Corset Company.

My mother thought Aunt Blanche had a romantic interest in Clifford Sprague, who worked at the post office and, like Blanche, had been widowed young. Uncle Frank thought there was something vaguely crooked about it—not on Aunt Blanche's part, but on the part of someone else—someone using an anonymous post office box, maybe, and trying to peddle nonexistent real estate or gold mine stock to foolish widows.

Typically, no one ever asked for an explanation—probably because no one would ever allow himself to be driven by Aunt Blanche. My mother was usually willing to ride with her, but since Mother thought she *knew* the reason behind the post office stop, and wanted to encourage the romance of Aunt Blanche and Clifford Sprague, she said nothing for fear of upsetting the applecart.

Of course Louis would have asked, and would have accepted any of the above reasons, or any other reason, or, as it finally turned out, the *real* reason, without batting an eye, since his own reasons for doing things rarely had much to do with the logic of a situation.

But we almost never got inside Aunt Blanche's car. "We'd never see you again," my father always told us. "Is that what you want?"

To Louis and me this was both mysterious and intriguing, and we kept hoping for some combination of broken-down cars and urgent errands that would require us to be driven by Aunt Blanche. There wasn't much chance of this though—the only car which was consistently broken down or smashed or pushed in was Aunt Mildred's, and the only errands Mother considered urgent were those involving medical emergencies . . . in which case she would obviously not call on Blanche, lest Blanche haul the victim (bleeding or choking or giving birth) first to the post office and then all over town.

"I think I'm the only one who's really comfortable riding with Blanche," Mother often said, and this was true. Neither of them was ever in a hurry to get anywhere, or dismayed to end up at an unexpected destination. "We always have a good time," Mother said . . . and even after the misadventures connected with her Uncle John's funeral, she insisted that it had been a pretty ride to get there, despite the complications.

This Uncle John was a relative unknown to Louis and me: The first we heard of him was through a telegram, delivered to Mother over the telephone.

"Uncle John Lane has died," she told us, "in Springfield, and the funeral is the day after tomorrow. He was my father's brother," she went on, "and I knew he was at a nursing home in Springfield, but no one's ever heard from him, or anything about him, so that's all I know."

How could this be, I wondered, in so nosy a family? This was my father's first question too when he heard the news.

"I just don't know," Mother said. "Nobody knows. Frank thinks maybe he had a fight with my father years ago. Rhoda said maybe he got wounded in World War I and just never came home. Mildred never heard of him.

"Of course we're all going to the funeral." She hurried right on, handing out reasons for this as if she were dealing cards. ". . . last of his generation . . . must be nearly a hundred years old . . . some of us *have* to show up . . . Mildred says we owe it to the past and to the future. . . ."

Perhaps Mother considered this lofty thought the last word in reasons, but my father did not. "Mildred!" he said. "Mildred just wants to go to Springfield."

"Well . . . what's wrong with that? She's never been there. I've never been there. The children have never been there."

"You're not going to drag them all that way!"

"Why, of course," Mother said. "They're the future."

Louis said later that this worried him a lot—he was afraid it meant that someone was going to point us out at the funeral, make us stand up, maybe even recite something about life. Still, he wanted to go. We both did—"all that way" sounded to us like foreign travel.

The arrangements turned out to be difficult. Of those who wished to go, only two were willing to drive.

"Let me guess," my father said. "The tortoise and the hare."

"I suppose you mean Blanche and Mildred," Mother said . . . but she did not deny that they were, in fact, the very ones, and my father said he might just as well drive himself, that otherwise he would sit home and worry.

He ended up both driving and worrying, though, because at the last minute an extra cousin appeared, and in the ensuing scramble for seats (especially seats in our car) Mother was seen to climb in with Aunt Blanche, who immediately took off (presumably for the post office), while Mother stuck her head out a window and called, "We'll see you along the way!"

There had been some talk of forming a caravan, in which the three cars would stay together, but my father said he would have no part of it, and discouraged everyone else from such a plan. "If Mildred is the number-one car," he said, "you'll lose Blanche at the first traffic light, and if Blanche is number one, you'll never get there."

Nevertheless, he became increasingly uneasy as time passed and we saw no sign of Mother and Aunt Blanche along the road. "Don't know where they are," he muttered from time to time, ". . . all going in the same direction on the same highway."

The late-arriving cousin, Howard Grashel, picked up this mood and kept saying, "Seems like the earth swallowed them up—seem to you like the earth swallowed them up?" till my father finally said, "For heaven's sake, Howard, shut up. You'll scare the kids."

But Louis and I didn't think there was anything to be scared about, believing, as we did, that grown-ups (even the grown-ups related to Mother) could take care of themselves. Had Mother been riding with Aunt Mildred we might have been scared, for Aunt Mildred passed us—honking and waving and then disappearing in the distance—"Like a bat out of hell," Howard said.

My father seemed to feel better after that. It reminded him, he said, that it was better to be late to a funeral than to require one.

"What happens when you're late to a funeral?" Louis asked me, for he was still fearful of public recognition. "Do you just walk in, in the middle of it? Do they stop while you walk in and sit down?"

"We're not going to be late, Louis," my father said. "It's your mother who's going to be late, unless they stop somewhere and take a taxicab."

To everyone's surprise, this was what they did.

At the very last minute, as we stood outside the funeral home, looking up and down the street for any sign of Aunt Blanche's Ford sedan, a blue-and-yellow taxicab pulled up at the curb and out of it stepped Mother and Aunt Blanche.

"Let's go right in," Mother said, hurrying up the steps, "I'll explain everything later."

"At least explain the taxicab," my father said.

"We were so late—it seemed like the best thing to do—Oh! . . ." She smiled. "Look at all these people. Isn't that nice?"

There were a lot of people, all very old, and all, naturally, strangers to us except for Aunt Mildred and her passengers.

"I hope Mildred thought to tell the minister who we are," Mother whispered.

It was immediately clear that Aunt Mildred had done so, because the minister based his entire remarks on the fact that so many had come so far to pay final tribute. He talked about life and death, and generations, and the old and the young (here Louis scrunched way down in his seat) . . . "Mildred and Rhoda," the minister said, "Frank and Grace and their families . . ."

When it was over Mother went to thank the minister, but my father said it ought to be the other way around, that he should thank us. "Makes you wonder what he was going to talk about before we showed up," he said.

To our surprise Mother came back right away, looking distracted, and hurried Louis and me out ahead of her. "We're not going to the cemetery," she said. "I told him we had to get right back. He understood. Where is everybody? Let's get out of here."

"They're outside," my father said. "What's the matter with you?"

"Oh!"—Mother rolled her eyes—"I didn't know what in the world to say! Fred, that's not Uncle John in there!"

"What do you mean?" My father stared at her. "Who is it?"

"*I* don't know!"

"Well, didn't you ask the minister?"

"Why, I couldn't say anything to the minister! I couldn't ask him, 'Who is this?' He just preached his whole sermon about us being the family!"

There was a lot of discussion and disagreement: Was this the right funeral home? Had Mother misunderstood the telegram? "How do you know it isn't him?" Aunt Rhoda demanded. "You never saw him. None of us ever did."

"I saw pictures," Mother said. "He was a little,

short, bald man, and this is a big tall man with lots of hair and a beard."

While everyone argued about what, if anything, to do, my father went back in to talk to the minister, who was surprised and puzzled, but found a silver lining to it all. He said that Mr. Johnson (whose funeral we had just attended) had no family at all, that his mourners were simply fellow residents at a nursing home, and that since we were all children of God and therefore kin, our presence was in no way inappropriate.

Aunt Mildred and Aunt Rhoda seemed willing to let it go at that. For one thing, Aunt Blanche was beginning to worry about her car, which was parked at a restaurant called Randolph's Ribs. "They were all very nice," she said, "trying to give us directions, and then calling us a cab and all . . . but they're not going to want my car sitting there all day long."

Mother said she'd never heard of such a thing, and now that we were here, we were going to locate Uncle John Lane, dead or alive, if it took a week.

Fortunately it only took my father about twenty minutes to figure out, and to confirm, that there had been some mix-up at the nursing home, inhabited by both Uncle John Lane and Mr. Johnson.

"They don't know much at that place," he said,

"but they do seem to know that *one* of them is deceased, and the other one isn't." He also said that he intended to call someone to account for this outrageous mistake, but Mother wouldn't let him.

"That sounds as if we're mad because he isn't dead," she said; "and anyway, these things happen all the time."

"That is simply not true," my father said—but of course he was in the company of people to whom such things *did* happen all the time, and they bombarded him with examples: "Remember Pauline . . . took the wrong baby home from the hospital?" "Remember Lloyd's dog Vergil that got listed in the telephone book, and after that got all the mail and the phone calls?" "Remember Audrey? . . . Calvin? . . . Maxine?"

Aunt Mildred summed it up. "Happens all the time, Fred."

"Not to me," my father said . . . but he had no wish to sue the nursing home, or to take Uncle John Lane out of it—for it proved to be a bright and homey place—so he settled for firm assurances that such a thing would never happen again.

Uncle John Lane turned out to be just what Mother said he was—a little, short, bald man: very old, very cheerful and very deaf, who said he was glad to see us and invited Louis to help him do his jigsaw puzzle. "It's a picture of some dogs," he said, "or the Rocky Mountains—hard to tell."

After a flurry of explanations and introductions, Mother and Aunt Rhoda tried to decipher the mystery of Uncle John, but they didn't have much luck. They had to yell, and neither one really wanted to yell about family matters for everyone to hear—and besides, Uncle John said yes to everything.

"I hope it wasn't a misunderstanding about money," Mother said, and Uncle John nodded. "That's right." "Political argument?" "That's right." "Heard you just never came home after the war. . . ." "That's right."

Louis, still doggedly assembling the puzzle, mentioned what was to him the most interesting feature of the day. "We went to your funeral," he said; and Uncle John nodded and said, "That's right."

"He just doesn't remember," Mother said finally, "and what difference does it make, anyway?" She raised her voice. "We're just all so glad we've found you. My goodness, the oldest member of our family! . . . And from now on, we're going to stay in close touch."

But as we were leaving we heard Uncle John ask a nurse, "Who in the hell were all those people?"; so my father said he didn't think Mother should count on much correspondence back and forth.

We all had dinner at Randolph's Ribs—"Seems only fair," everyone said—and headed home, after some reshuffling of people.

"I still think I ought to ride with Blanche," Mother said. "I'm not sure Howard knows the way."

"I don't know what difference that makes," my father said. "*You* were supposed to know the way, and look what happened." He wanted to hear all about what had happened, he said, and Mother could start from the time she stuck her head out the window and said, "We'll see you along the way."

"Well," she began, "it was a really pretty ride. . . ."

Louis and I listened for a while to a bewildering account of side trips to get gas and lunch and fresh country eggs, of misinterpreted road signs, of inaccurate directions from people at bus stops and grocery stores, of detours—"There were no detours on the highway," my father said; but it seemed that Aunt Blanche and Mother were not on the highway often, or for very long. It had been an eventful day, though, and Louis and I fell asleep somewhere south of Xenia and didn't wake up again till we were home.

My father was right about Uncle John Lane. He never answered any of Mother's letters, but the director of the nursing home did send monthly reports about his health and well-being. She also sent us a small package containing Mr. Johnson's personal belongings; photographs, Confederate money, five Zane Grey westerns, a collection of travel postcards, and other odds and ends.

My father said this had to be the last straw in confusion, but Mother thought it was nice and eventually came to refer to Mr. Johnson as a distant relative, and—even more eventually—just seemed to forget that he wasn't one.

Perhaps, in her mind, he took the place of Aunt Blanche's secret post office flame, Clifford Sprague, who got married (to someone else) and moved to Indianapolis, much to Mother's consternation. She wanted to know what went wrong between him and Aunt Blanche but didn't like to ask, until my father pointed out that Aunt Blanche was obviously not heartbroken and, in fact, seemed unmoved about the whole thing.

"Clifford Sprague?" Aunt Blanche said, when she was questioned. "I didn't even know him. Whatever made you think I did?"

When Mother reported this conversation she said everybody was wrong—that Blanche didn't care who read her postcards, and wasn't about to buy more real estate, when it was all she could do to get the grass cut and the hedge trimmed on the real estate she already had.

"There's a perfectly simple explanation for why

she always goes to the post office," Mother said. "That's how she learned to drive. She just followed the mailman around his route—first one mailman, and then another one. They always started at the same place and came back to the same place, and they never went very fast. It was perfect for Blanche, and it just got to be a habit."

"Now let me understand this," my father said. "Blanche would get in a car, and . . ." But then he stopped. He had finally realized, I guess, that he would never understand this, any more than he ever understood Mother's driving habits, Louis's contest entries . . . Aunt Mildred or Genevieve Fitch or Vergil the dog—any more than he would understand similar events and revelations yet to come.

Instead, he said, "It's the craziest thing I've ever heard . . . so far."